**Some people run from danger...
Ava Crowley flirts with it.**

When Ava and her brother embark on a trip to TerrorCon, a horror movie convention in Oklahoma, chaos follows. The kind that involves blood, sexy vampires, brooding hunters, and even a renowned demonologist. But Ava and the hunters aren't the only ones searching for answers.

Cassius is pulled back into a world of blood, lust, and death, a life long forgotten. In order to help clear a dear friend's name, he must travel to Oklahoma, all while fighting a magnetic blood bond between him and the snarky vampire slayer he can't live without.

Will Ava and Cassius be able to fight temptation surrounded by blood and lust?

Blood & Lust is book two in the Ava Crowley, Vampire Slayer series, filled with snarky heroines, sexy-as-sin monster hunters, and other seductive supernatural beasts.

Blood & Lust

Ava Crowley, Vampire Slayer

Book Two

Copyright ©2022 Ariel Dawn

ISBN: 978-1-77357-423-3

978-1-77357-424-0

Naughty Nights Press LLC

Cover Design by Willsin Rowe

BLOOD & LUST

AVA CROWLEY

VAMPIRE SLAYER

BOOK TWO

ARIEL DAWN

NAUGHTY NIGHTS PRESS LLC • CANADA

Love is a smoke made with the fume of sighs;

Being purg'd, a fire sparkling in lovers' eyes.

—William Shakespeare

Love isn't soft, like the poets say.

Love has teeth which bite and the

wounds never close.

—Stephen King

CHAPTER ONE

AVA WATCHED THE doorstep from the comfort of her Chevy Impala.

She leaned one arm on the window, her cheek resting on her fist, while her other hand stretched out, fingers tapping against the steering wheel.

She'd expected more... something.

Everything seemed quiet in the sleepy town of Chester.

The town was no longer the center of media frenzy.

Sure, there were still *murders*, but nothing quite as scandalous as attractive college kids with strange marks on their thighs and necks, like the Chester Murders two years ago.

She could have sworn the man she'd followed had *all* the signs of a vampire, and even if she didn't believe it to be so, her vampire radar never lied.

The bite mark she'd sustained only two years prior—the bite that saved her life—flared with heat while her skin prickled with goosebumps every time a vampire was near.

As if she could have willed it with thought alone, her wrist heated, and a soft knocking on her passenger window alerted her.

Her lips twisted in annoyance as a rather attractive blond with a penchant for leather pants smirked at her.

Cassius.

"What do you want?" she bit as she tried to look around him.

"May I come in?" He held a coffee in his hand.

Though she knew she should say no, she could not bring herself to do so, and that aggravated her.

"If it means you are no longer going to obstruct my vision, then, yes, by all means, enter my humble abode," she drawled sarcastically as she heard the click of a door.

Cassius opened the door and slid into the passenger seat, the motion accentuating his long legs—and the curve of his ass—in his black leather pants.

Ava pretended not to notice.

Especially when her blood *heated* at the sight.

"I was once told never to attend a stakeout without coffee." Cassius offered her the coffee cup.

Ava raised an eyebrow as she took the coffee from his hands, quickly opening the lid. The scent of vanilla and cream was divine.

"I was told never to invite a vampire into your house or car, yet here we are." She took a sip of coffee and had to admit it was divine.

"Thanks for the poison, but you didn't have to—"

"I was in the neighborhood." Cassius's eyes sparkled with amusement.

"Uh huh. Sure..." Ava rolled her eyes, focusing on the doorstop.

Nothing.

No movement.

Cassius casually leaned back in the seat.

"What if he does not show?" His voice was smooth, like caramel.

"He'll show," she answered as she took another drink of the sweet liquid.

"But if he does not..."

"Then I go home," she grumbled.

"But you will not rest, will you, Ava?"

She closed her eyes, letting the coffee warm her insides. She refused the idea that anything but the coffee could warm her like *this*.

"Until I put a stake through his chest, you mean? No, I won't."

Cassius sighed, turning his head to

look out the window.

"Well, I suppose we wait then."

"There is no *we*, Cassius. This is my life, and—"

The door budged and Ava sat straighter.

"Bingo," she said as she set down her coffee, turning her car off.

CHAPTER TWO

THERE WAS NOTHING Cassius could do about Ava's extracurricular activities. He understood her reasons for slaying those like him; after all, it was his kind who killed her boyfriend, Ross. It was his kind that left her for dead; would have bitten, fed on, and killed many others without her intervention.

But he was not like those other vampires. He did not wish to kill, or maim, or indulge in the many pleasures vampires could indulge in without fear of retribution.

He had saved her life with his bite, with his venom, and though he knew she could dust him at any moment *if* she wanted...

She hadn't. She had threatened to do so on more than one occasion, but she had not moved to do it, and he had not made any move to finish his claim, to turn her. He hadn't made any indication toward her that he was interested in consuming her, either.

It seemed they were at a standstill. But as he sat in Ava's car alone, he could feel her pulse alive within him, and he had to admit his weakness.

He'd watched her drive a stake into a rogue vampire only two years ago. The black blood of his kind sprayed on her pale cheeks, across the creamy expanse of her cleavage, her eyes alight with adrenaline and power. A power that reminded him of someone else.

They are not the same.

Cassius shifted in his seat, yet his gaze did not leave the entrance of the door Ava had walked through. Though he hated that she put herself in danger on an almost constant schedule, he also knew he had no way of truly stopping her.

The bite that he had given her had undoubtedly changed both of their lives, and the repercussions of that bond affected them both quite differently.

For starters, Cassius could feel her

pulse within his own veins; a feeling he had grown rather fond of in the last two years. Yet, in her presence, his blood heated as if he were a boiling pot, and she the fire. In the beginning, it was startling, but now... Every fiber of his undead body being lit up like a star in her presence, pulled him to her like an unyielding force of gravity. The fight was becoming much more difficult.

"What are you doing?" he mused aloud to himself as his gaze stayed fixed on the entrance. He wasn't sure if he was talking about himself or Ava.

It seemed to be getting harder to separate his desires from those of the bond they shared.

As he sat in her car, surrounded by her intoxicating scent of jasmine and bergamot, Cassius worried his control was slipping.

His phone vibrated in his pocket. When he did not answer, it vibrated again. Incensed, he relented and pulled it out of his pocket.

"Yes," he snapped.

"Where the hell are you?" The voice on the other end of the phone was one he knew well, but not one he'd shared his phone number with.

"I believe I do not have to disclose my whereabouts to you, Malcolm." Cassius breathed deeply.

"I swear to God, if you're with her..."

"I can assure you, your sister is safe." He noted a flicker of light in the window.

"I know what you are, Cas," Mal's tone was cut and dry.

"A vampire? A little late for that discovery, isn't it?" Cassius kept his voice controlled.

"An Aurelia."

Cassius stiffened at his surname.

"And what do you plan to do with this information?" Cassius could not help the desperation in his voice. The last thing he needed was Malcolm to tell Ava he was the last of a fabled bloodline among the covens. He'd spent so many years trying to escape his name, and all that came with it.

Death, heartbreak, and immortal misery.

When Ava looked at him, she didn't see an Aurelia. He wasn't sure what she saw truly, as she was quite cantankerous most of the time, but she certainly didn't see him as the bounty he knew he was. Had she known, she would have certainly staked him without a second thought.

For the Aurelian line was cursed with the gift of life.

The rate of born vampires had dwindled ostensibly since the rate of vampires with the ability to sire seemed to be lessening. Above all, there was only one line which could bear descendants by birth, or by blood.

His.

The last of his bloodline would die with him. That much he'd promised himself. He would not burden anyone with a claiming bond, with the curse of immortality. And he certainly wouldn't burden anyone with a child.

A child who would be cursed to end up just as he had.

No, it was quite safer to stay hidden, blend in.

To leave his past in the past.

"If I told you, I'd have to kill you," Malcolm snickered.

"Yes, well, forgive me if I have to decline your offer."

"I'm going to find a way to break your bond," Mal said with conviction.

"There is no way—"

"There is *always* a way," Mal's voice echoed through the cell phone, and then the sudden click was deafening.

Cassius nearly jumped as Ava climbed into the car once more, black blood spattered on her jeans, some on her shirt.

Her skin was free of blemishes, though.

"Don't you have anything better to do than sit in my car like a fucking stalker?" she bit as she started the engine.

"Perhaps, I prefer your company," he answered honestly.

Ava rolled her eyes. "And I prefer a well aged Bordeaux and a man with a pulse, but when life gives you lemons..." She looked in the rearview mirror and backed up rather quickly for Cas's liking.

I have a pulse...

He wanted to defend her allegation, but what could he say?

He had a slow, dying pulse that belonged to him, but he had hers, too. Even at this moment, he could feel its elevation, the adrenaline still running through her.

He could feel her fear, her excitement.

Her lust for such things.

It stirred dark things in his own

being, and he had to force the thoughts far away. For when they started their onslaught, there was only one way to truly quiet them.

Cassius shifted in his seat, stifling his rigid erection. This close to her, the scent of jasmine and bergamot was overpowering, and the feel of her pulse in his veins—alive with excitement—was like a thrall of its own.

He knew how Ava liked to make her kill.

How she liked to get close enough to her prey they could sink their fangs in her neck.

She was more than a slayer.

She was the spider, and he was nothing more than dead in her web.

So he said nothing. Instead, he leaned his arm out the window, and turned his face to the moon, praying the crisp air would cool the fire that surrounded him on all accounts.

CHAPTER THREE

AVA STOLE A glance at the stunning vampire in her presence. Against the black interior of the Impala, his flawless skin illuminated by the moonlight, he looked positively angelic.

Golden blond hair blowing ever so faintly from the gentle breeze that crept in through the window. The planes of his face were soft as if he was no younger than she was; barely twenty.

But she knew he was much older than he let on.

Though, she'd never asked. Such things didn't really matter and would only make things more difficult when the time came to put a stake through his heart.

And undoubtedly, she would put a stake through his heart.

Because he was a monster.

Like Brody, the vampire who'd slit her legs and left her to bleed out on the floor.

Like Liam, the vampire who killed her boyfriend, Ross.

Like the vampires who killed her parents.

Yet, Cassius had made no move to

feed off her, or turn her. Instead, he brought her coffee and donuts. Instead, he showed up out of nowhere, swooping in to dismantle her plans. He always dismantled her plans, whether he meant to or not. Because no matter what, when he walked in the room, her skin chilled with goosebumps while her blood boiled beneath the surface, and her pulse quickened.

And when she looked at him—

Bad idea, Ava.

You know better.

Ava forced her gaze back on the desolate road. The radio flickered between stations, and she reached for the dials just as Cassius did.

His fingers brushed hers with the lightest of touch, and she noted they didn't feel cold and dead.

They felt soft and warm.

She pulled her hand back as if he was a flame and she'd been burned.

Cassius cleared his throat as he turned the dial. Songs faded in and out until he'd settled on a station. The dark beats filled the car as the singer crooned on about holding someone's hands in the holes of his sweater.

Ava scowled, but she didn't change the station. The bass thumped, while the deep, breathy sounds of the singer filled the space.

She stared at the road and refused to acknowledge the thickening fog surrounding her while the singer droned on as she shifted in her seat, feeling strangely flush.

Which had nothing to do with Cassius.

No, she was just keyed up from a fresh staking.

When she pulled up the driveway, the headlights shone on the empty garage.

Cassius was out of the car within seconds, opening her door.

She flashed him a gaze of annoyance, but he only had the audacity to look just as charming as always. Like some picture-perfect leading man in a romantic comedy, or something out of a cheese-induced dream.

She wanted to say a hundred things to him, but all she could do was truly get as far away from him as possible. His visits were becoming much more frequent, and she worried that perhaps he'd started to get the wrong idea. Their *bond* did not make them friends. In fact, it was quite the opposite. There wasn't enough coffee or Danishes in the world to make her forget the reality of *what* Cassius was.

What he'd done to her.

What he'd probably done to several other people throughout his long life.

She stopped at the door, sliding her key into the lock. She could feel him behind her, but he kept his distance. He always kept his distance.

As he should.

"You can go, Cas." She huffed as she stepped across the threshold of the door and turned on the light. She nearly stumbled over her duffel bag and suitcase by the door.

Fuck, Connie must have moved them.

Cassius's gaze flicked down to the luggage.

"Are you leaving?" She didn't miss the

sadness in his voice.

"Not that it's any of your business—" She leaned against the doorframe, crossing her arms.

"But, yes. I'm leaving town for a few days." Her eyes searched his, gauging his reaction. His glowing green eyes looked hurt. As if her words alone could cut him like a knife.

He just wants your blood, Ava.

Nothing more.

"I see," was all he said as he stood on the other side of the threshold, in the cold autumn air on her front porch.

He wouldn't dare cross it without her permission.

Not because he couldn't, but because, as he once pointed out, it would be rather rude to insist on coming inside when he was not wanted.

"Where are you going?" Ava watched as he slid his hands into his pockets, the motion jostling his leather pants just enough to be noticeable in the lamplight, casting shadows on his pale skin.

"Again, not that it's any of your business, but..." She twisted her lips. A part of her screamed to shut the door on him. She didn't owe him anything. He had saved her life, with his bite mark, but she had not known the cost of such things. The bond between them was nothing more than circumstance.

Cassius was not her friend.

He was the *enemy*.

Who happens to look quite appealing in leather pants.

But Ava found herself divulging her plans far too easily to Cassius, despite wanting to keep them to herself.

"Oklahoma." She pursed her lips and imagined locking them up and throwing away the key.

"What's in Oklahoma?" Cassius smirked at her.

Ava felt her shoulders relax only slightly.

"TerrorCon." She smiled.

"What is... TerrorCon?" He raised an eyebrow, looking perplexed.

"Only the biggest horror convention in the United States." Her eyes glittered with excitement.

"Horror movies, you mean?" Cassius tilted his head to the side.

"Yup. It's five days of pure horror."

Cassius twisted his lips.

"That sounds awful," he chided.

"It sounds like heaven," she said as her lips tugged into a smile.

Cassius hesitated, and she turned, seeking her moment. But for some reason she couldn't shut the door.

"When do you leave?" His voice stopped her.

"Tomorrow." She turned once more and took in his lovely features. Ava had the startling concern that Cassius would not let her go. Such a thought was unnerving to her, and instantly flared her defenses, her panic.

"Don't follow me," she ordered.

"I would not—"

"I mean it, Cas." She stood her ground. She'd told him so many times to leave her be, but he always came back. Before she could hear any more of his sweet, decadent voice, she shut the door.

CHAPTER FOUR

CASSIUS WALKED THE empty streets alone, with only his thoughts for company. Thoughts of amber eyes and luscious pink lips as they gazed back at him only moments before her cutting blow.

Ava was leaving.

It is not as if she is leaving you.

Of course, that was not the case at all—but Cassius could not deny the sharp sting in his heart at her words. Since the night he bit her, he'd barely been away from her for longer than twenty-four hours.

Not that she knew that, of course. He'd gone to great lengths to appear in her proximity sporadically. But every night it was the same routine. He'd venture close to the estate and check to make sure she was safe and sound.

On the nights she'd have nightmares, he'd creep in through her open window, and he would be there, offering the gentlest of touches along the back of her hand until she relented back into a quiet slumber.

He would find his way to the piano bar on the nights it became too unbearable to be near her. Anything to pull his attention away, make him forget even for the slightest moment that his life was no longer his.

That he was as much as marked as she was.

Those nights were becoming much more frequent, much to his dismay.

He longed to touch her, more than a gentle caress of his fingers on her skin. To feel her blood as it pulsed beneath her skin, to feel the soft flesh against his palms. Against his lips.

How could my father stand this?

Cassius knew his father had claimed his mother's blood before turning her, but seven years?

How did the thirst, the *need* for her not drive him completely insane?

Because they were together.

In love.

His thirst for her blood may not have been fed, but they'd had you...

It was obvious the other main need of a vampire was being met.

The thought made Cassius somewhat jealous. It had been a good twenty-five years since he'd been intimate with anyone, and his diet of corpse blood wasn't exactly the most fulfilling. Perhaps, that was why the desire was so strong, but alas, he refused to partake in feeding on a live human, or in casual sex, blood induced or not. He would not give himself and his Aurelian curse to someone he didn't love.

Not after Eden...

He wished the cold autumn air would cleanse him, but he knew better.

Nothing would cleanse him of Ava

Crowley.

No, nothing could chase such a siren song away, and yet she thought he was a *threat* to her.

It had been two years.

Two years of fighting a blood bond that was maddening, yet somehow, he had remained controlled. He had not stepped out of line once, and he never would. Not unless she asked him to, in which case he would most certainly oblige.

But the way she had regarded him, when she told him he was leaving...

How she commanded him to stay away.

As if he would go against her very demands, but only moments before...

She seemed at *ease* with him. Those moments, as infrequent as they were,

were exactly the thing that kept Cassius from going mad. Deep down, below the bitterness, and the sarcasm, the threats to end his existence...

She felt it, too.

The magnetic pull that had *nothing* to do with the bond.

But Ava Crowley's life was etched in blood and bones. Her world shifted on its axis the night Liam and his cohorts killed her boyfriend and left her to die.

In the wake of it all, she was reborn.

A hunter.

Like her brother.

Like her parents.

He knew it was asinine–it went against all the codes and made absolute perfect sense–she would despise him and what he was. That one day, she would truly end him.

Yet, all of his life Cassius strived to be more than what he was admittedly born to be.

As he walked through the dark doorway of his residence, he knew Ava's wishes were founded in truth. Despite the fact she'd started to move closer to him, that he caught her stolen glances at him... the truth was still bright and clear. There was quite an obvious divide, and Cassius knew he must stay on one side of it. The thought of her being so far away—far enough away he couldn't feel her pulse, couldn't smell her intoxicating scent— Made his slow beating heart tighten in his chest.

Perhaps she is right to put some distance between us.

Perhaps this is for the best.

Cassius quietly slipped out of his

heather-gray shirt and leather pants and folded them neatly before setting them on the armchair in the corner of his bedroom.

The cool air kissed his fair chest, the shadows playing over the expanse of his toned abdomen. He ran a hand through his hair and took a deep breath.

Images of Ava filled his brain, of the car ride home.

Her fingers as they brushed his skin, sending bolts of electricity through his entire being.

Thankfully, she had pulled away, but the action left him feeling a sense of sadness.

As if she was repulsed by his touch.

Cassius did not need sleep, but he crawled into bed, anyway.

The quiet of the night was most

comforting, and he knew he was alone.

Tajiri and Jasmine would not be home until dawn.

So he let the thoughts come unabashedly in the welcome solitude.

Her deep eyes of fire as they fixed on him, speckles of black blood across her cheek, in the corner of her ruby red lips.

Legs straddling Liam, stake in his chest.

Her cleavage spilling out of her tight corset top.

His eyes closed, he did not fight the memory.

Crimson streaks spilling out of her creamy, pale thighs, the look of abject terror on her face, streaks of mascara and tears staining her perfect cheeks.

The feel of his fangs piercing her soft skin, and the way she gasped.

His thrall begged to wrap itself around her, his thirst clamoring to be met.

It was only a drop. A small, minuscule drop of blood that ran down his fangs, simmered on his tongue.

Hot, sweet.

Cassius slid his hand beneath the waistband of his boxers, and the memories replayed like a song on repeat.

The sound she'd made when he bit her, that stirred a deep instinctual desire within him.

Every stolen touch: a brush of a finger here, a side-by-side touch of her arm or leg, or bump of her shoulder, sent little shockwaves throughout his being, heated his blood.

Ignited a thirst within him that even blood couldn't quench.

His breath hitched, and the feel of her

pulse—its steady rhythm within him—made him feel warm all over.

Images in his mind flashed of perfect, pink lips; lips that housed a sharp tongue no less, traversing over his, biting, sucking at his before making their way down his neck. He quickened his movements on himself, feeling the familiar tightening in his muscles, his desire culminating like a whirlpool. Building and building with each thought, each fantasy, each memory spiraling into thoughts of what he longed for.

The thought of that sharp tongue he'd grown so fond of sliding across his, licking his fangs. Leaving trails of warm saliva down his neck. Tracing the shallow, toned lines of his hips...

Cassius stifled his groan of release

into his pillow as a mixture of relief and guilt overcame him.

He closed his eyes as he tried to catch his breath, his heart beating a fraction faster than it normally did. Coupled with Ava's pulse, the feeling made Cassius feel almost human again.

Five days.

That was less than a week.

Surely you can manage that...

Though, as Cassius left his bed to wash up, pushing through the familiar feelings of guilt, he knew it was a lie. But for Ava's sake, he would find a way to manage. After all, he'd managed hundreds of years without a mate, and thus far, two years without giving in to the pull of the bond.

Yes, five days would not make a difference.

At least, that was what he told himself before he allowed slumber to overtake him.

CHAPTER FIVE

AVA SMILED BRIGHTLY as Mal threw her duffel bag in the backseat. His hair had gotten longer, covering his ears; a true sign that it had been far too long since she'd seen her brother.

"Ready to get this fucking road trip started?" He looked positively as giddy as she felt.

"Abso-friggin-lutely!" she said as she settled into the passenger seat of his red Chevelle.

The car actually smelled clean, like fresh laundry detergent.

"You cleaned the car? For me?" she teased.

"A man has to keep his house in order every once in a while, right?" he jabbed back at her.

It wasn't entirely a lie.

Mal lived his life split between hotels, motels, and his car. Such was the nature of a musician and a hunter.

Mal was both.

He'd started to leave for much longer periods of time, ever since discovering Ava had been bitten.

She understood his reasons.

After all, finding a way to break her

bond with Cassius was his priority next to finding the vampire who had killed their parents.

He chased dead end leads all while working tirelessly with his partner, Jake Dallas, and his hunter friends—Vinny, Tito, and Hunter—to eradicate the world of the evil bloodsuckers.

And the quest for answers, the promise that came from wielding a stake into the chest of those monsters... well, Ava understood its pull completely.

Still, she couldn't deny she missed her brother and had been looking forward to this one on one time with him since he'd brought it up only a few months prior.

There were eleven years between them, but despite the age gap, they had always been close. Growing up in their home in Massachusetts, with their parents, had been a happy, fulfilling life.

Eating junk food on the oversized couch with her brother, curled up in blankets, watching movies like *Halloween* and *A Nightmare on Elm Street*—in the dark—were some of her most favorite memories of her childhood.

While most children favored the likes of princesses and cartoon animals that talked, Ava preferred the thrill of a good horror movie. The way the anticipation built, drawing her to the edge of her seat until the scary part came and made her jump.

And strangely enough, it had been those films that helped her through the darkest moments of her life. Her parents' deaths. Moving to Chester to live with her aunt.

Becky Lee Michaels did not care for such things as scary movies. She only cared about the finer things in life.

Mal started the car up, and the radio blared loudly, and Ava couldn't help but smile.

"I hear Skeet Ulrich is going to be there," Mal said flashing a smile.

Ava squealed with delight.

"I'm definitely meeting him, if that's the case." She could hardly contain her excitement.

"I heard they have a zombie run!" she said as she settled into her seat, ready for the long drive.

"They have a Carrie-style prom, too," Mal's voice hitched an octave as well.

"This is going to be so much fun," Ava said as she leaned against the window and watched all of Chester pass by in a blur.

***

The Silver Starling Hotel was quite ominous looking, set against the gold and orange hues of the setting sun. It looked less like a hotel and more like a haunted mansion.

It had been a long eighteen hours cooped up in Mal's car. They'd taken turns driving, naturally, but sleeping in Mal's car was not all that comfortable.

Her muscles ached as she stood on the pavement, her red skull suitcase and black duffel slung over her shoulder.

Mal arrived next to her, sans suitcase. He lived out of a backpack, anyway.

Ava had to appreciate the beauty of the fabled hotel. Tales of ghost sightings and stories of the many things it was used for throughout the ages had always intrigued her.

It looked as if it housed a plethora of secrets within its walls.

The inside, however, was not as beautiful as the outside. On the outside, it looked positively elegant, but inside it had been renovated to reflect a modern age. Stale blue carpet, a lounge with tiers of continental breakfast offerings, and slightly worn rubbery chairs.

The lobby was busy for eight p.m. Visitors bustled about as she watched the room.

Mal handed her a room key. "There's been a bit of a mix up and they actually booked us for two rooms, but I figured you wouldn't mind," he said as he started off in the direction of a hallway.

Ava followed quickly, dragging her skull suitcase behind her.

"There really is a God," she teased.

Mal scowled. "Really, Ava?"

"Would you have preferred a sock on the door instead?" She smirked.

"Oh my God, Ava!" Mal's voice hitched an octave and she laughed.

"I'm kidding, Mal, take it easy."

"I'm going to need to scrub my brain now, thank you."

Ava chuckled. Their rooms were right next to each other, as luck would have it, but Ava was still thankful for her own privacy.

"I'm fucking beat. Think I'm going to turn in early so we can get a head start tomorrow on the opening festivities," Mal said as he leaned against his door, twirling the key in his fingers.

"Okay." She shrugged.

"You should do the same." He raised an eyebrow.

Ava smiled. "Of course."

***

Hamlet's Bar was decently packed for a Wednesday night. Ava had heard that many of TerrorCon guests liked to partake in liquid refreshments the day before the convention, mingling with the guests. She wondered who she would see there, perhaps she'd run into Skeet Ulrich and get her picture. Maybe share a drink.

Who cares if he's old enough to be my dad, he's still fucking hot.

She'd forgone her leather jacket and band tee for the night, and instead, had opted for a black *Creature from the Black*

Lagoon top with the sides cut out, a pair of tight black jeans, and her studded boots.

It didn't take long before some man—dressed in all black with more chains than an oil rig—offered to buy her a drink.

Which she gladly accepted. It wasn't as if she was incapable of purchasing her own. After all, she did have a fake ID. But at least she wouldn't have to pay, and if a man got too handsy expecting payment other ways, she kept her stake on her at all times. As well as pepper spray and a switchblade.

Ava downed her whiskey rather quickly, and her skin prickled with goosebumps.

Her wrist flared with heat, and she felt a startling feeling.

Like she was being watched.

She looked around the room inconspicuously, but she could not fathom where the vampire was in such a dense crowd. Or if there was more than one.

Her gaze caught on a man across the bar, surrounded by a throng of women. Dark eyes set amidst his olive skin, a hint of stubble peppered along his jaw. His black hair was short enough it curled around his ears, but long enough for him to have swept it into a messy coif. He held a beer in his hand, his red button-up sleeves rolled up to his elbows, a few select buttons unhooked. In the red light of Hamlet's, he looked absolutely devilish. She recognized him almost immediately.

Sam Kingsley.

The controversial demonologist from the show *Hell on Earth.*

Ava contemplated walking over and saying hello, but her thoughts were interrupted by a sheer wind that left her skin with goosebumps.

She turned without thinking and followed her vampire radar like a bloodhound.

And perhaps in a way, that's what she was.

For it was the black, slick blood running down her stake that she chased.

The fire as it consumed bones and supernatural muscle, disintegrating it into nothing more than ash to be swept away in the wind.

Her senses heightened, but her vision blurred only slightly, and Ava found herself out in the cold midnight air of Ansley, Oklahoma, in a patch of dark forest.

Lured like the unfortunate mortal such creatures thought she was.

"Hello," she called out, her heart pounding in her chest. She knew he was out there, and she knew without a doubt he'd make himself known if he thought she was but a frightened, innocent little thing.

Ava waited impatiently for him to make his appearance.

But all hopes of staking a bloodsucker went out the window when she heard a shrill scream, coming from the direction of the bar. Instinct overran her, as she turned and ran out of the woods and into the arms of danger once more.

CHAPTER SIX

CASSIUS DID NOT need an alarm or device to wake him up, as his internal clock always seemed to know when the sun had risen. Like the waves of the ocean moved in tandem by the draw of the moon.

He opened his eyes to the sunlight that poured in his room, and he knew it was still quite early. But the morning felt quieter than usual. Where the chattering of birds was usually heard this deep in the woods, there was nothing. Nothing but the near whisper of tree branches scratching against his window.

He sat up, stretching his arms, and the soft blankets fell from him, highlighting his fair torso. It was then he noticed that he felt... *empty.* His slow heartbeat still ticked away in his chest, yet...

He felt different.

Because the pulse he'd gotten used to feeling in his veins over the last two years was suddenly gone.

Because she is gone.

He pushed himself out of bed and forced himself to move. Lying in bed and moping about things he had no control over, or rather a slayer he had no control over, was not good for anything.

He quietly padded his way into the kitchen, nearly tripping over something on the floor. When he looked down, he sighed in exasperation.

In the midst of their return home, it seemed Jasmine and Tajiri had lost their clothing piece by piece in a rather unkempt trail of breadcrumbs. Cassius picked up the lump that was Taj's jeans and chucked them at the couch.

The kitchen, it seemed, had stayed clear of any of the remnants of Taj's and Jasmine's dawn arrival.

Thank heavens for that.

Cassius focused on the motions of his morning routine, taking note of the details if only to distract himself.

The sound of coffee percolating, the

sizzling of bacon grease in the skillet. The flaky texture of his chocolate croissant.

He sat on the barstool, his bare feet touching the rims as he swiveled back and forth. A loud, mechanical chime sounded, the sound of his phone going off once again.

He debated leaving it, just in case it was Malcolm calling to harass him once more, but when he saw the number was one he recognized, he picked it up immediately.

Especially because he hadn't heard from the owner in quite a long time.

"Leon... how..."

"It's not Leon," a soft, sweet voice spoke on the other line, and Cassius froze.

"Cora?" He hadn't heard Cora's voice

in ages. Since he'd left Oklahoma…

"I…I didn't know who else to call…" He could hear what sounded like a faint sob.

"Cora, what's wrong?" He tensed immediately.

"It's Leon… I…I think he's in trouble."

"What kind of trouble?" Cassius pressed.

"There was a murder, but I *know* he had nothing to do with it!" She let out a wail.

"You and I both know Leon is not capable of such things," he tried to reassure her.

"I think someone is trying to frame him…"

"Whatever for?"

"The club…" She sniffled.

"What club?"

"The Dark Hearts Club, of course." Cora said the name as if Cassius should have known.

But he didn't. He'd left in haste all those years ago.

Twenty-five years ago, to be exact.

In the middle of the day, without a word to anyone... Except for Leon.

He'd preferred it that way, for he wasn't certain who he could trust. He needed to be as far away from the Boracelli Coven as possible.

Far, far away from the vampire who had betrayed him.

Eden Boracelli.

"What makes you think I can help?" Cassius spoke as he readied about the kitchen, cleaning up his dishes rather quickly.

"Because you're the only person I can

trust. I know you care for him as I do..."

Cassius made his way to his bedroom once more, opening drawers, pulling out clothes.

"Where are you?" he asked as he pulled a suitcase out from his closet. He hadn't used it in over twenty years, and it was covered in dust.

"Ansley." Cora's voice seemed to have calmed itself.

"Ansley..." he pressed. "Oklahoma?" Cassius's heart stilled, which was no small feat considering it was a slow beat to begin with.

"Yes," she answered softly.

Oklahoma is a large state, I doubt it is in the same place Ava is visiting.

Do not get your hopes up.

"I will inform you when I arrive. Do not tell *anyone* I am coming. Even Leon.

Do you understand?" He brushed off the dust from his suitcase before opening it.

"I understand," she said.

The phone went dead, and Cassius was left alone once more.

He knew, better than anyone, that Cora would not have called if the situation wasn't serious.

She knew just as well as Leon did that Cassius valued his privacy, that he wished to stay under the radar. Yet, he'd all but shone a damn spotlight the moment he marked a dying college girl in Boracelli territory, so perhaps fleeing Chester would be the smart thing to do to get his head right. If Ava could leave, so could he. At least, that was what he rationed.

His friend was in trouble and needed his help.

Eden had said once that he always had to play a hero, and perhaps she was right.

For Cassius did not have to think twice before he zipped up his suitcase and headed for the train station on the first train to Ansley.

CHAPTER SEVEN

"AVA LOOK OUT!"

Ava heard a voice holler from her left. Before she could even get a good look, she collided into a solid mass.

"The hell..." She recognized the solid mass too little, too late.

"What the fuck are you doing here?" She stumbled backward only slightly as large, muscled arms held her at bay.

"I could ask you the same thing." Dallas looked at her with curiosity.

Ava looked around his lumbering frame, toward Hamlet's.

Toward the sound of the scream.

"I don't have time for this... There's—"

"Ava, what the hell—" Vinny said as he came upon Dallas's behind.

Dallas's fingers gripped her arm, his grasp firm and warm against her chilled skin.

"You're supposed to be in bed!" Mal's voice cut in.

Ava looked at Dallas, and Vinny, and then to Mal.

"So are you!" She broke Dallas's hold and readied her stake.

"You still didn't answer the question." Dallas crossed his arms, his bright blue eyes looking her up toe to head, his gaze strangely… possessive.

"Well, I was hunting a vampire, then I heard a scream and—"

"For the love of all that is holy—" Mal ran his hand over his face.

"And I was on my way to—"

"Ava, no one's there." Vinny took a step toward her.

"You don't know that, I just heard—"

"We just came from the same direction. Tracking a vamp. Probably the same one you were. There was no scream." His gray eyes were soft, his lips pursed.

"Oh hell no, I know what I heard!" Ava crossed her arms.

"Have you been drinking?" Dallas raised an eyebrow at her, his lips turning up in the corner only slightly.

"I'm not drunk, if that's what you're implying. Takes a hell of a lot more than one glass of whiskey to get me tipsy, thank you very much." She scowled at him, and for the moment imagined setting his annoyingly sexy smirk on fire.

The memory of just how enticing those lips could be came flooding back to her, and she pushed them down.

Now is really not the time.

"He's gone, probably scared him off." Mal spun his blade around like it was nothing more than a toy, his brown eyes carrying a hint of disappointment.

"That's because the lot of you are louder than a fucking freight train." Ava pushed past Vinny, knocking him in the shoulder.

Dallas sighed behind her as she approached Mal.

"This is supposed to be a trip for *us*. Not us plus the fucking Goon Squad."

"It wasn't supposed to happen like this—" Mal huffed as he headed toward the strip where Hamlet's stood out like a sore thumb.

"Forgive me if I don't believe you," she grumbled.

"It wasn't! Dallas and Vinny were tracking a vamp from upstate. They followed the trail here, that's all."

"Oh, so it's just a coincidence that the vamp led them straight to the freaking town where TerrorCon is? Maybe he's dying to check out the guest list?" The sounds of the bar carried, getting louder with each step.

"Yes, Ava. Not everything is a damn conspiracy theory." Mal slid his hands in his jean pockets.

"Although, if you think about it, it's the perfect place to find victims who are into that sort of thing." Mal cocked an eyebrow at her, and Ava didn't have to ask what he meant.

Though they didn't speak of it often, he'd been more than crystal clear in his concerns Ava would give in to the blood bond and fall for a tall, lean vampire with a penchant for leather and eyes like the brightest emeralds. She scoffed in response, rolling her eyes.

Never going to happen, Mal.

Trust me.

"Well, he's not likely to come back out now that we've spooked him, so it's as good a time as any to call it a night," Vinny interrupted them.

"Where are you guys staying?" Mal asked as he lit a cigarette.

Ava watched as he blew smoke into the cool air.

"The Silver Starling," Dallas answered. In the light of the neon signs, his muscles rippled in orange and red glow. The shadows fell on his expanse of skin from the open sides of his muscle tank, and as he shifted just a fraction. Ava could have sworn she saw the points of a star tattoo on his right pectoral.

A sight that immediately brought back images of just how taut those muscles were, the black lines standing out against his skin. The memory caused her to flush, even if it was only momentary.

"Funny, that's where we're staying." Ava shot Mal a suspicious glare.

"What are the fucking odds?" Mal grumbled between puffs.

***

Ava tossed and turned in the hotel bed. It wasn't terribly uncomfortable. In fact, it was a king size bed with rather soft bedding. But even if it had been made of clouds, Ava would not have been able to rest.

For her mind swam with thoughts of screams, chilled skin, and a solid slab of abs.

"Tomorrow, Ava. You need to sleep. Can't very well be looking like death if you want to rub elbows with all the guests at the con tomorrow," she spoke the words aloud to herself.

Still, she couldn't fathom the serendipitous occurrence that put Jake Dallas in her path once more.

It had been two years since she'd last

seen him. While Mal had ventured home in recent months, Dallas's presence was not to be found. He'd always traveled with Mal, and his sudden absence was startling to Ava.

Why did she care if he came home with her brother, at all?

Because you like playing with fire, that's why.

Truth be told, just because they'd shared a kiss—a very hot kiss to be exact—did not mean they were bound to one another in the slightest.

Yet, Ava could not help but wonder if their secret kiss had anything to do with Dallas's sudden lack of availability.

The way he'd gripped her arms in the forest, smirked at her with those deceptive blue eyes, as if he was challenging her to make a move.

Challenging her as he had in the boxing ring of the Bat Cave. To anticipate his movement.

Well, two can play at that game, Jake.

CHAPTER EIGHT

AVA SCANNED OVER her appearance in the hotel mirror, a long oval-shaped thing that appeared older than it probably was. Still, she was thankful for a full-length mirror so she could take in her look from top to bottom.

It was only the first day of the convention, and thus, she had decided to try and keep her outfit simple, and comfortable. Her costumes wouldn't make their debut until the sun was down... as long as the vampires kept themselves at bay long enough for her and her brother to enjoy themselves.

She smoothed her hands over her overalls, one strap left unbuttoned in the haphazardly dressed look which seemed to pull her casual *Chucky* outfit together.

A knock on her door pulled her from her thoughts as she finished putting on her lip gloss.

When she opened the door, it was not who she expected to see.

Instead of Mal dressed up as Michael Myers, Dallas stood there. He leaned in the doorway, his blue eyed gaze traveling over her body, leaving her with a sudden warmth that both annoyed her and intrigued her.

"Morning, Kitten." He smiled.

"What the fuck do you want?" She twisted her lips as she braced her arms against the doorway, blocking him from any further entrance. He looked just the same, standing in dark wash jeans, and a Jack Daniels muscle tank. His tan arms exposed, as always, showing off his pentagram tattoo and a new addition which looked like a black cat with a crescent moon in between its eyes underneath it.

Interesting.

"I was heading down to the lobby to grab some breakfast. Thought you might want to join me."

"And why would I want to do that?" She narrowed her eyes at him.

He had the audacity to laugh. A low,

dark chuckle that made Ava nearly stop breathing for a moment.

It had been two years.

Two years since she'd discovered the monsters in the shadows. Since she'd trained with Dallas.

Since they'd kissed.

She could still remember the taste of his tongue in her mouth, his hands as they coursed over her, touching her everywhere.

Though Ava was not looking to jump from fire to fire, she could not deny such a kiss had diluted all the chaos, even if it was only short-lived.

For when she kissed Dallas, she felt *nothing*.

No thoughts of Cassius, no memories of bloodied bodies in the corner of a frat house basement, no knowledge of vampires and other creatures of the night.

All she could feel was *him* against her thighs, his searing lips against hers.

She let herself wander into the darkness, lost in all the unsaid words and unspoken desires that clearly existed in the space between them no matter how hard Dallas insisted against it.

Dallas's words broke her memories once more.

"Because I know how you get if you don't have your daily dose of sugar and caffeine."

The way in which he smiled was rather flirtatious. Ava could not hide the smirk on her lips as she turned away from him. She would not let him see.

As if perfectly on cue, her stomach

growled. Rather loudly for her liking.

"Fine. But this is purely out of survival alone," she said as she left him standing in the doorway. She dug around in her suitcase to retrieve her crossbody bat purse.

While she knew he should stay in the doorway, a part of her wanted him to follow her inside. Wanted him to come in, lock the door, and kiss her again. Run his hands over every inch of her. Fill her head with *nothing*, to take out all the chaos and replace it with fire...

Focus!

She threw on her purse quickly and hurriedly escaped through the doorway, past the attractive lumbering hunter in her way.

She did not wait for him to catch up. Instead, she kept her pace quick.

"If I didn't know any better, I'd say you're *not* happy to see me," he said teasingly as he caught up to her stride. They walked down the neutral-toned hallway, a silent race to the elevator.

"And what makes you think you know better?" she said as she grabbed hold of her purse strap. Gripping it tightly as she refused to look at him and his sexy, smug face.

As she came to the elevator, she pounded the down button impatiently.

Dallas's body slowly enclosed her proximity, and before she could even have time to process it, the doors dinged and opened.

She hurried inside and mashed the buttons just as he entered the space. Once the doors swished closed, it was just the two of them.

Dallas hit the hold button and the elevator stopped in place, before taking his spot next to her.

Although he only stood next to her, with an ample amount of space no doubt, she couldn't deny that her heart was pounding.

It's from the run to the elevator...

Not.

But Dallas's voice broke her thoughts as he put himself in front of her.

"Because of this..." He slowly encroached on her space, and Ava's body heated in response. He was only inches away from her, his arms leaning out, hands gripping onto the elevator bar on both sides of her, and she was trapped.

But being a prisoner of Dallas's gaze, the way he was looking at her...

It was so radically different than he had been two years ago when she'd last seen him. Hesitant to even kiss her, at first.

He leaned closer, his lips only a fraction away from hers, and every bone in her body told her to fight back, to yell and scream at him, yet she couldn't find the words.

She also felt the instinct, the desire to close the space between them and kiss him until she couldn't breathe.

"If *I* meant nothing to you, Ava, you wouldn't have blinked an eye when you saw me."

"It's been two years, Dallas. You had your chance." Ava looked up at him, taking in the sight of him, all the finer details. His bright blue eyes, chiseled jawline. Dark hair that looked shorter than she remembered. His full lips. Despite the thirteen-year age difference between them, he still didn't look a day over twenty-five.

All the familiar warnings came flashing back.

He's too old for you.

He's your brother's best friend.

Ava tried to push the thoughts away.

She felt her heartbeat quicken as she moved to release the hold button, but he stopped her by stepping in her way.

"Two years I've been fighting to try and forget you... forget what happened between us... because I thought..." He licked his lips and reached out his hand, pushing a strand of her dark hair behind her ear.

"What did you think, Jake?" she breathed as her heart pounded away in her chest. She could not break his gaze, and she could not deny that his touch felt more than welcomed.

"I thought... I thought maybe *you'd* gotten over it. Regretted it, maybe?" Dallas's gaze dipped to her lips, and Ava couldn't help herself.

She'd never been good with self-control, or regrets. And in the presence of Jake Dallas, both seemed to evaporate completely. Even after a two-year absence. It was as if they were right back where they had started, the elevator becoming a boxing ring.

Ava fell into his kiss, savoring the taste of him on her tongue once more. Her entire body melted, and the embers of yesterday sparked once more.

Dallas's hands found her hair, his fingers twisting her locks, pulling her closer.

She parted her lips, settling her hands on his hips, her fingers grazing over the open expanse of his skin, visible from the loose open sleeves of his muscle tank. Close enough, she could feel him harden against the flesh of her exposed thighs, and the realization only made her wish for more.

To see how far he'd let her go.

Yet, the image that filled her head as his lips caressed hers was a shocking splash of cold water to her system. One that she'd become all too familiar with in Dallas's absence. It seemed any time Ava decided on partaking in any kind of romantic pleasure, the thoughts were always there to douse her with their chilly remembrance.

Memories of glowing green emeralds,

of soft lips on her wrist, surged forth. Of her blood rushing to the surface, of a hot tongue searing her wound.

Of Cassius.

No, this isn't supposed to happen...

Last time...

The images she'd tried to keep locked away rushed to the forefront with new intensity.

The very *thought* of Cassius's angelic Calvin Klein-model features elicited a soft moan from her lips, and she hated that it did so. Hated that he'd taken this from her, too. There was nowhere she could escape the looming presence of Cassius.

He was everywhere.

She hated that his thoughts pervaded her consciousness night after night, day after day.

Dallas did not know that, and instead he responded to the sound of her desire by trailing his lips over her jaw.

The memories of the night Cassius bit her melded with ones that never happened, and ones she knew *could never* happen. Ones Ava couldn't help but think of in the dead of night, alone. In the crevices and cracks of her dreams and nightmares. Ones that she could only quiet with a touch of her hand and regretful release.

Cassius's lips biting at hers, his soft tongue and lips leaving trails of ice and fire along her neck, her breasts, biting at her nipples, his fangs pulling back to show the hint of a smile she found sexy as hell.

She fought the thoughts the only way she knew how. The only way she'd been fighting them for two years.

"Dallas..." she groaned into his mouth as she wrapped her arms around him, deepening their kiss, her tongue eagerly seeking out his, letting her hands travel down his chest, settling at the waistband of his jeans.

She needed this.

Touch.

Release.

To chase the ghosts away that haunted her thoughts.

To chase *him* away, the vampire who marked her.

And then, as if her thoughts could speak of their own accord, Dallas stopped his motions.

He stopped, looking her over once and he just... walked away and pressed the hold button.

Ava was left dizzy from the onslaught of feelings, thoughts, her head spinning from Dallas's sudden departure from what would have been a rather lovely way to start the day.

He stepped aside and cast her a smug smirk.

"I'm happy to see you too, Kitten."

"Fuck you," she bit, her fingers wiping her mouth of the remnants of Dallas on her lips.

The elevator doors dinged, and Dallas exited the space.

***

"What's your deal, you've been in a mood all day? I thought this trip would, you know, make you *happy, not* pissy," Mal said as he sat down in one of the many chairs in the empty panel room.

"I am happy, she bit.

"Are you still pissed about last night?" he asked curiously.

Ava crossed her legs and sipped on her iced coffee. "You could have told me you took on a job," she said as she flashed a disapproving glare at her brother. Attendees filtered into the empty room, lining up in the seats.

"I wasn't *supposed* to be working a job, so there was nothing to tell." Mal crossed his arms and kicked his legs out, crossing them at the ankles as the rest of the attendees filled in the spaces of empty chairs.

"I won't be mad if you let me in on it."

"Ava..." Mal sighed.

"Practice makes perfect."

"I can handle it," he rebutted.

"I know you can. But I want in." She

held her ground.

In the light of day in the hotel, she could see Sam Kingsley's face much better.

He looked less like a devilish creature and more like a sexy lumberjack in the flannel shirt he was wearing over his Van Halen shirt.

Mal did not respond to her inquiry, and she knew he wouldn't. He still wasn't entirely on board with her interest in staking vamps. He'd trained her, along with Dallas—with the intent that she could *defend* herself should the situation arise, especially given the circumstances surrounding her claiming. But he had not anticipated that she would be *good* at slaying vampires all on her own. That she would search out the bloodsuckers of her own accord and disintegrate them into ash.

The doors shut on the panel room with a loud thud that echoed in the expansive space, and the chatter in the room quieted.

Ava focused her attention on Sam Kingsley and the moderators of his panel, abandoning the conversation at hand with her brother.

It seemed like an eternity of rehashed information as the moderators reiterated Sam and his story. How he'd gotten into the study of demonology, the success of his show, *Hell on Earth.* He'd answered the questions with finesse and even a smile. But something about the way in which he did so, Ava thought there was an air of annoyance in his voice. As if he detested such events as this.

"We will now open the floor to

questions, but please keep them short, and to the topic of this panel. No personal questions about Mr. Kingsley's life, please."

Mal huffed. "Only people with shit to hide say that," he grumbled next to her.

"Maybe he just likes to keep his *work life* and his *personal life* separate, unlike some people I know," Ava bit back.

The string of attendants started to line up in front of the microphone, but no questions would be asked.

As the doors slammed open and in walked three police officers, and TerrorCon security, all while making quite the entrance.

"This panel is over, and all of you are to return to your rooms at once," the officer spoke loud and clear, and chatter erupted once more.

He bellowed louder, and the chatter turned to silent hushes.

"There has been a murder at this convention. Please, remain calm and return to your lodging."

Ava's eyes widened and Mal pursed his lips.

"Ava..."

"It can't be a coincidence..." she whispered to her brother as the room erupted into chaos once more.

"Mr. Kingsley, please come with us," another officer spoke plainly at the table.

"Of course, officers. Anything I can do to be of assistance."

As Sam quietly stepped down from the stage, Ava could not help but steal a glance at him, and she could swear for only a moment his eyes glowed red.

CHAPTER NINE

CASSIUS STEPPED OFF the train into the murky, dull station. He looked around the concrete building, which was not as busy as he imagined it would be. Then again, it had been a long time since he'd last visited Ansley...

The memories pushed forth and he could not squash them, for there was no pulse to distract him and he was alone.

Eden scowled in disgust at the small station.

"If this station is any inkling of the town we are looking at, I don't like it already."

"What is wrong with middle America? Is that not the ideal location for happy families?" he asked curiously.

"I prefer something with a little more taste."

"I know what you prefer." Cassius's lips turned up in a smile.

"The covens will expect more," she sighed as Cassius reached for her hand with his free one.

"The covens expect us to look the part, Eden. If we at least look like we are trying to make a family—"

His voice trailed off and he could not

finish the sentence.

Eden stopped and turned to face him.

"I know you have as much at stake as I do, I am sorry, I—"

Cassius dropped the bags at her uncharacteristic show of vulnerability. He settled a hand at her hip gently. Careful not to push, to ease her strain only slightly. Neither of them had asked for this arrangement.

An engagement.

It wasn't a proposal of love in the least.

With his father dead, his mother was left alone and in danger from many enemies. She'd done the only thing she thought she could to keep herself safe. She'd approached the very coven, the very woman who'd forced her and his father out to begin with.

Isabella begged for forgiveness and protection in exchange for what Francesca had long desired. An Aurelian stud to unite the Boracelli bloodline and create the perfect vampire.

Eden had fared no better; forced into the arrangement because of her ties to the late Marcellus Medici. Though the extent of their ties had not been disclosed to him at the time, even Cassius knew he would have said yes regardless. To keep them safe, both his mother and Eden.

He'd considered her a friend, at least. Arranged marriages happened all the time, after all, and some were not as lucky to even know the person beforehand. It was not an ideal situation in the least, but the arrangement was for more than just a wedding.

They needed to produce an heir; a

legitimate one. Or, at the very least, as Eden had claimed, look like they were doing everything they could do as such.

Something that should have come rather easy to the both of them, given their long-standing friendship with one another.

But neither seemed to be able to treat the engagement as anything more than a death sentence.

But perhaps it did not have to be that way, Cassius thought.

Friends become lovers all the time. At least, that was what he believed from all the years he'd studied mortals, befriended them. Read their literature.

Friendship could very well be the foundation a good marriage was built upon.

And with nothing but time on their

hands, perhaps...

Perhaps, one day it would be love.

The clock sounded with a large chime, pulling Cassius from his thoughts.

"Cassius!" the lilt of a young, feminine voice called to him, and he could not help but smile. She looked different than he'd seen her last.

While Cora had always bore eternal youth, being forever sixteen, he had to admit she looked much older in the modern day.

Her once bountiful red curls were now poker straight, mixed in with thick golden blonde streaks. Her bright blue eyes still sparkled like the sky on a sunny day, and her complexion was as pink as ever.

She's fed recently...

Cora all but ran toward him, her pointy black heels clattering against the dull, unswept floor. She threw her arms around him, her round breasts squishing up against him in a tight hug.

Cassius lightly hugged her before removing her ever so gently.

"Cora."

"You look just as I remember!" She squealed in delight. "How long has it been?"

"Too long, I am afraid. Although, I cannot say the same for you, my dear." Cassius shifted his stance as Cora collected herself.

"Yeah, well, when in Rome... you know," she said as she flashed her baby blues at him, running her fingers through her waist-long locks.

"Do you like it?" She smirked.

Cassius was not sure how to proceed with compliments when it came to Cora.

While he cared for the girl, being his best friend slash pseudo father figure's adoptive daughter and all, he did not wish to stoke Cora's insatiable crush.

He'd always known she fancied him.

But Cassius did not see her as anything but a fond family friend.

A child, even, given Leon had taken her in and considered her such.

Leon never married or claimed a mate. He'd lived alone, an eternal bachelor, until he had stumbled upon a dying young prostitute in the middle of England. She'd been bitten, but it seemed her sire had been disposed of by hunters, and as his body lay dying, decaying—Cora was in dire straits.

Leon sealed her wounds himself and

took her in. He'd always wanted a child, but as his inclinations were toward men and he was not an Aurelia, producing an heir was not in the cards for him. Taking Cora in had changed many things for him; suddenly the rumors of his predilections ceased.

"If you like it, that is what matters most," he answered.

Cora frowned only slightly. "I thought you liked long hair."

"What I like, my dear Cora, should be of no interest to you," he said politely.

Cora rolled her eyes and motioned for him to follow her.

"Why must you always be so bloody noble?" She sighed.

Cassius followed her outside the train station to a limousine that lay in wait.

"You did not have to bring the

cavalry, Cora. I said to remain low key."

"Cassius, Cassius, when will you accept that you deserve the finest things in life?" The driver opened the door for her and she slid in, her eyes never leaving his as she pat the seat next to her.

He languidly slid in as the driver took his luggage.

When the door closed, he felt strangely overwhelmed by the scent of chemical freesia.

"My dear, when will you discover that the finest things in life are not things you can buy."

Cora smiled, her ruby red lips stretching sweetly.

"Everything and everyone have a price, Cassius. Even you."

CHAPTER TEN

AVA LAY BACK on Mal's bed, staring at the ceiling.

"The one time we actually get a chance to do something fun and it's over before it even began."

"I would have thought you of all people would be most excited about a murder at a horror convention," Mal sighed.

"I would be more excited if I could leave my hotel room and hunt some fucking vampires. Or murderers," Ava huffed.

"And here I thought you wanted to spend time with your dear old brother." A knock in the door interrupted them both.

Mal slowly ambled to the door and Ava leaned up on her elbows.

"Dallas..." Mal didn't seem particularly excited at the arrival of his partner.

"Where's the rest of the Ghostbusters?" Ava said, not taking her gaze from the ceiling.

"Tito and Hunter were headed down to Hamlet's for a drink. Vinny is out on patrol," Dallas said gruffly, and Ava could feel his presence like a poltergeist, even though she was certain he was far enough away he could not see the rise and fall of her breath as it quickened from his voice alone.

There'd been plenty of times the memory of Jake Dallas had crept into her dreams, popped up unannounced in her wandering mind. But Ava was no fool, and she did not expect Dallas to show up on her doorstep, begging to sweep her off her feet.

A kiss was only a kiss, no matter how delicious it was.

It wasn't a relationship, and she would not delude herself into thinking Dallas wanted more. But then he showed up at her door and boxed her in in the elevator, kissed her with desire, a hunger that she couldn't deny, and for once she was glad Mal stood between them.

For Ava was not certain what would happen if it was just the two of them behind closed doors.

"I thought the place was on lockdown?" Mal said, perking up.

"That's what I came to tell you. Seems word around the hotel is they've got nothing. Just stirring up shit to try and see what comes up. They had nothing on that Kingsley guy, he was out in minutes 'Cause he lawyered up."

"Figures," Mal grumbled.

"What about the convention?" Ava said as she sat up, looking at the two hunters.

"What about it?" Dallas settled his eyes on hers, and Ava couldn't help the flutter in her stomach at the sight.

The way he looked at her was as if...

As if he, too, were glad to have a buffer.

"Please, tell me they're not going to cancel..."

"Nope. No canceling. But there will be a curfew. I guess they're changing the hours or something. Con hours will end at like six, or something, through Monday."

"Oh thank God!" Ava said with relief.

"Well, that's good news for us. Means we can hunt this thing in peace," Mal said as he got up and headed toward the cooler, grabbing a cold bottle of water.

"You want one, Dallas?" he asked nonchalantly.

"Sure," Dallas responded, just as the bottle nearly missed his head. He caught it so quickly, Ava could actually see the breeze rustle his hair.

"Well, shouldn't be a problem as long as *some people...*" He shot Ava a smirk before continuing. "As long as some people can keep quiet."

"Fuck you, Dallas," Ava shot back as she rolled her eyes.

Dallas let out a dark laugh.

"I bet you couldn't stay quiet to save your fucking life," he taunted her.

"Unlike you, I know when to keep my mouth shut." She huffed as she got up and headed for the door.

"Where are you going?" Mal asked.

"To Hamlet's. I need a drink."

***

Ava tossed back another shot of whiskey.

Hamlet's was packed with bustling

congoers all worked up about the "bust" that never was. It was all anyone wanted to talk about in the damn place. She'd already started to tire of the "where were you, what were you doing when..." discussions no sooner than she arrived. She hadn't even seen Tito or Hunter, despite Dallas's claims they'd gone to have a drink. Perhaps she was too late.

Why she let Dallas get under her skin was a mystery to her.

She was usually so much better at dealing with cocky assholes like Dallas. They were a dime a dozen on campus, not to mention she'd been a cheerleader in high school; a label that brought with it plenty of assholes in the wake of her pom-poms.

But there was something about Dallas, about the way he spoke, the way he looked at her, that made her want to put him in his place, but also...

There was something about Jake Dallas that called to some deep, dark corner of Ava that she didn't quite want to acknowledge.

So, instead, she drowned the thoughts with shots of whiskey.

What would Cas think?

The thought was intrusive and came out of nowhere, startling Ava. She opened her eyes, slamming the shot glass down on the bar so hard from the shock she thought it may break.

What the hell?

Why would I even care what Cas thinks about... anything?

Even the thought of the vampire seemed to make her blood rush. Though, the scar on her wrist did not flare with heat as it usually did. Instead, she found herself slightly chilled as images of his hurt expression on her porch filled her brain. The sight of such things left her feeling guilty, as if causing the vampire pain of any sort was... wrong.

Ava cleared her throat, her gaze catching the bartenders once more.

"Can I get another one, please?" she said boldly. She did not want to think about Dallas or Cassius. Not now. Not here. Though, it seemed the further she tried to run from them, they always followed, showing up in the darkness as she lay in bed, in her wandering daydreams.

The bartender nodded in response, and Ava let out a deep breath.

"Where's your boyfriend?" A cool voice pulled Ava from her wayward thoughts.

She turned to see a familiar face, and as her gaze settled on the man, the scent of fire and teakwood filled her pathways. It was a most masculine smell, and it was rather divine to Ava's senses. Paired with the dark, inviting eyes and boyish grin on Sam Kingsley's face, Ava couldn't help but gasp in awe.

"Ummm... I don't have a boyfriend," she said sweetly as she swiveled on her barstool toward the delectable demonologist.

"You were in the front row at my panel with that guy, I thought..."

"You thought what?" Ava said with a smile, feeling the effects of her whiskey and her natural confidence mingling together to heighten her boldness.

Sam Kingsley may have been a celebrity, but he was still at the base of all things, a regular man. A man with an extensive knowledge of the supernatural who was also quite attractive, smelled heavenly, and was hitting on her.

"I thought a woman as beautiful as you would *have* to have a boyfriend."

"Does that line work on all the girls, Mr. Kingsley?" Ava said with a sexy smirk.

Sam leaned on his defined arms against the bar. Ava could see the shape of his muscles all along the curve of his shoulder, the slight outline of his chest through the flimsy black t-shirt he wore.

"Call me Sam," he said, flashing her a smile. "And no. I know what you must think, a guy like me travels all over the place and picks up girls in every city, but I can assure you that is the furthest thing from what my life is like."

"Oh really, Sammy, do tell me how utterly boring and unaffected your super-cool life really is," Ava said with a chuckle as the bartender dropped off her shot.

"Is that what you want to hear about? My boring life? No theories on cryptids or creatures of the night? Or about the murder looming over this convention?" he said with a raise of his eyebrow.

Ava felt a strange feeling in her stomach at Sam's words. Her head felt slightly hazy, likely from the alcohol, and she half-considered telling him everything.

The truth about who she was.

What she was.

A slayer.

It was a truth she hadn't admitted to anyone, not even her closest friend,

Ember.

Sam waved at the bartender authoritatively.

"The last thing I want to talk about is fucking bloodsuckers," she drawled, noting the sparkle in Sam's eyes.

"Thank heavens. Most of the time that's *all* people want to talk about with me. Exorcizing demons is my *job*, but it's not who I am, you know?" he said with a deep sigh, his shoulders relaxing. Ava had to tear her sights away from the man; the look of vulnerability on his face was too much for her.

His dark hair fell in his eyes, the mixture of blue and red lighting from the bar casting shadows on his boyish features.

Her skin prickled with goosebumps and a shiver ran down her spine, like a splash of ice water.

"Unfortunately, I know *exactly* what you mean," she grumbled. The bartender made his way over to them, catching Sam's attention.

"I'll have one too, thanks," Sam demanded; the bartender nodded back in response.

"I didn't catch your name, *bellus*," he said as he angled himself closer to her.

The motion caused Ava's blood to heat even if only a fraction, and her insides felt tingly. Ava rolled her eyes, not at all impressed by Sam's compliments. But for the moment, she did not care about the demonologists' social skills, and she engaged him, anyway.

After all, was this not what she wanted?

To go on an adventure far away, to forget the sinfully delicious vampire who had gotten too close?

To meet new people, discover new experiences?

"Call me Ava," she responded with a wink as she raised the glass the bartender finally dropped off alongside Sam's.

"Beautiful name for a beautiful woman," Sam said, flashing her a smile. "Very well, *Ava*. What should we toast to?" The lighting of the bar and throughout Hamlet's had shifted into a smattering of red and orange hues as a band took the stage, readying to play.

When the beginning notes of "Bark at the Moon" filled the air, Ava couldn't help herself.

"How about... cheating death," she

said with a laugh. "To living to hunt the monsters another day."

"I can definitely toast to that," Sam said with a grin.

CHAPTER ELEVEN

AVA'S BACK CRASHED against the wall as the door slammed shut. Sam's hands roved down her side, settling on her ass as he squeezed. Her head felt slightly foggy and warmth blossomed between her thighs as Sam pressed his hardness against her.

A giggle escaped her throat as she

grabbed him through his jeans, eliciting a deep growl from his throat.

"Ava..." he groaned, his hands finding their way up her back, into her hair. His lips crushed against hers and he tasted bitter, like whiskey and day-old coffee. But for the moment Ava didn't care.

There was only this moment.

There was only *him*.

The feel of his hands, of his dick rubbing against her through his constrictive jeans.

There was only the feeling in her stomach of growing arousal, and a deep *need* to sate the madness building within her.

To *forget*.

To lose herself in someone, so she could not feel the heat of her scar, could not think of glowing-green emerald eyes, or the memory of fangs piercing her skin.

Sex always did the trick to make her forget, even if the forgetting was short-lived.

"Let me guess, you don't do this sort of thing, normally, right Sammy?" she said darkly and bit her lip, looking up at him through hazy eyes.

Sam's hotel room was dark, and they hadn't moved to turn on the lights. Though in the darkness, she could still make out his fine features, and it only added to the spinning sensation in her head and body.

"I don't..." he whispered as he kissed her right below her ear. He moved his lips farther down her neck, stopping over the throbbing vein in her neck, a deep groan leaving him as he did so. "You smell so good...”

“I, um... need to use the bathroom,” Ava said as she took a deep breath. Something about the proximity of his body to hers, the way his hands gripped her, his voice...

Her entire body felt alive, but she was cold. Freezing, actually... and every ounce of her body begged to feel his touch, to feel the warmth of his body against hers, all over. Her head was spinning, and nothing was making sense...

“Of course,” he breathed deeply, the sensation of his breath on her skin causing her blood to heat.

Ava swallowed nervously as she backed away slowly, feeling her way to the bathroom in the darkness. When she found her way to the door, she entered, shutting the door quietly after turning on the light.

The room had been renovated, but it still retained some of its original charms in the crown molding, in the ornate pedestal sink's design.

Ava gripped both sides of the sink, forcing herself to look up at her reflection in the mirror.

Her short hair was slightly disheveled, her dark eyeliner smudged out slightly farther than the corners, and her lipstick had worn off. Likely, from the extensive kissing marathon they'd engaged in on the way back to his hotel room.

"What are you doing?" she whispered to herself in the mirror. The bright lights were jarring, and she had to blink a few times to adjust.

Ava turned the faucet on, splashing cold water on her face, if only to cool down. Her entire body felt flushed and warm away from him, as if she was boiling from the inside out.

Though she did not expect an answer—from her reflection or herself—Ava could not deny in the solitude of Sam's bathroom, she was certain of two things. The first was that this moment was a once in a lifetime moment.

The host of *Hell on Earth* was on the other side of the door, waiting for *her*.

The second was that something about the whole situation: the bar, the toast, the walk back to the hotel room—

I don't even remember the walk back to the hotel room, Ava realized as a knock sounded on the door.

I know I only had three shots...

"Are you okay in there? You're not sick, are you?" Sam's voice sounded from the other side.

Ava noted the slight concern in his tone, and her shoulders eased as she pulled her gaze from the mirror.

"No, I'm okay... uh... be out in a minute..." she said as innocently as possible.

Ava shook her head, the thoughts gone like dandelions on the wind. Her stomach flipped with anxiety, her nerves standing at attention.

That's probably just the alcohol.

She squared her shoulders, glancing at her reflection once more, and pushed it down. Forgetting all about her nerves, about her instincts. It wasn't like her to get cold feet, especially when it came to sex. Then again, Sam Kingsley wasn't some college frat brother or biology tutor with no shame. He was an established, thirty-something-year-old man who looked like trouble, and Ava *loved* trouble.

She sucked in a deep breath and turned on all her charms as she shut the faucets off and exited the bathroom into the darkness of Sam Kingsley's hotel room... like a lamb to the slaughter.

CHAPTER TWELVE

THE DRIVE TO Leon and Cora's home was longer than Cassius had anticipated. He sat stone still next to Cora, like a statue. She tapped away on her phone mindlessly, and for the moment he was glad. He rolled the window down only a hair, taking in the sights of the world as they passed him by.

Nothing looked familiar, but then again, he knew it wouldn't. It had been years since he'd been in the town, and historical landmarks, businesses, and establishments were falling through the cracks all across the United States, across the world, really.

A part of him was saddened by this, that the world he'd once known was buried underneath a layer of skyscraper and steel, that the ornate, romantic buildings and idyllic towns had all shifted into cookie cutter replicas of one another; indistinguishable.

I wonder if that donut place is still here...

Cassius's thoughts were interrupted as the car pulled up to Leon's house, and Cassius couldn't help but smile.

It seems as if some things will never change.

Leon's house looked just as he'd remembered. It was as preserved as the day he'd last seen it, as if time itself had evaded Leon and his microcosm.

Though Cassius was not prepared for the onslaught of memory that pushed forth through his thoughts.

Cassius sat on the veranda with a tall glass garnished with a small lime wedge. He wasn't entirely certain what alcohol it was, the liquid was as clear as water.

Leon smiled as he took a seat next to him, but Cassius could barely look up from his glass.

"I'm sorry about your father," Leon said softly.

"I know I should feel upset, or angry... or something..." Cassius sighed deeply,

closing his eyes. "But I don't."

"What do you feel, Cassius?" Leon leaned back in his wicker chair, resting his ankle on his knee, balancing his long, sinuous elbow on the arm of the seat, his kind eyes staring at Cassius as if he could see right through him, down to his very soul.

"Nothing," Cassius said as he ran his fingers up and down the side of the glass, feeling the cool condensation against his fingertips. "I feel nothing, Leon. I feel numb." Cassius took a sip of the drink, noting the prominent taste of lemon on his tongue and it reminded him of home.

"I know the two of you had a... complicated relationship, but I know without a doubt your father loved you."

"He left me, Leon. He left my mother

and me because he thought I was not his, and when he found out I was... I thought for a moment things would change, that we could repair what he'd broken, but..."

Cassius took a long drink, nearly emptying his glass as a mixture of emotion overcame him.

"I thought, perhaps, we could make amends, and maybe things could be like they were before. The three of us, a happy family... Well, five of us, really, if you counted Theodora and Sylvie."

Leon did not press him, only waited for him to continue.

"But he had to go back to the covens. Because somehow, some way, he'd been found out. His actions put us all back in the spotlight, and it was his actions that led him to his death. Led my mother to fend for herself with the only bargaining

chip she had."

"You," Leon said softly.

The words fell over him like a heavy blanket.

"I had no choice in the matter," Cassius said as he finished his drink. The remains of dusk fading into night.

"You always have a choice, Cassius. Even when it feels like the cards are not in your favor, you have the choice. It is just not always an easy one."

"I did not want to watch my mother struggle again without him. You know the man had his enemies, and now that he's gone... I couldn't risk it. I—"

"A noble notion from a noble son." *Leon leaned forward, pulling the glass from Cassius's hands.*

"But nobility is not always heroic. It masquerades as selflessness, as

martyrdom.

When there is no one left for you to fight for, Cassius, who will fight for you?"

Cassius blinked the thoughts away as the car pulled up around a cobblestone driveway, in front of a large Grecian fountain.

"It looks just as beautiful as I remember," he said in awe as the driver opened his door.

Cora looked up from her phone with a smile.

"Well, you know how much of a stickler Leon is about *preservation,*" Cora said with a roll of her eyes.

Cassius took a moment to take in the spectacular features of the Victorian-era home, from its wrap-around porch to the high windows and textured roofing.

A warmth blossomed in Cassius's

chest, and relief overcame him as he walked up the steps, following the driver who was carrying his luggage. As soon as the doors opened, Cassius could not help the smile that crossed his face.

He felt *happy.*

The winding staircase and its ebony railing, the parquet flooring that looked freshly waxed, the ornately-carved entry table which boasted a vase full of peonies and lilies freshly cut from the garden. The air smelled of flora and fresh wax, and the scent relaxed him in a way he hadn't expected, his shoulders easing up for the moment as joy settled in his stomach.

Though Cassius had called many places home over the course of his long life, none had felt like such. He looked around the preserved foyer, taking in the beauty of it all.

He felt as if he was finally *home*.

"Cora, sweetheart, where did you put my—" Leon's crisp, clear voice echoed in the entryway as he rounded the corner and stopped dead in his tracks as he looked at Cassius.

In many ways, it was as if he had not changed at all, but in so many ways, he was different.

His eyes were still the same, bright and sparkling in the artificial lamplight against his olive complexion, his dark hair swept back behind his ears. His glasses had changed, from the round academic ones to sleek, rectangular frames that made him look older, more refined. Though, he'd forgone his stuffy academic-style suits and traded them in for a simple pair of khakis and a blue button-down silk shirt. He looked more like a young golfer than an ancient vampire.

"My word, has Hell frozen over?" Leon said with a genuine smile.

Cassius could not help but return it with one of his own.

"Last I checked, no."

Leon walked with a steady pace toward Cassius, reaching out and pulling him into a tight embrace.

"It's been far too long, Cassius," Leon said as he hugged him.

Cassius's arms found their way around the man who did not look a day over thirty.

"I missed you, too," he said as he hugged him back. Once the shock of his arrival had worn off, he held Cassius by the arms a short distance.

"Do not get me wrong, I am overjoyed at your company, but I must ask... what exactly are you doing here?" Leon asked curiously, his gaze traveling from Cassius to Cora then back again. "I thought you were laying low, trying to—"

"Cora called me..." Cassius answered before Leon could finish.

"Whatever for?" Leon said, his dark eyes shooting up in alarm.

"She said you were in trouble, that there's been some deaths..."

Leon's face went pale, a feat for a vampire such as he.

"I... I have things under control," Leon said, his entire demeanor changing completely.

"No, you don't. You're too focused on your breakup, too wrapped up in your damn project to see that the club is in danger!" Cora huffed angrily.

"Leave Grayson out of this, Cora! Those deaths have nothing to do with the club!" Leon bit at her.

"Those deaths have *everything* to do with the club, Leon! You cannot trust your investors, I have told you, I—"

"Cora, leave us." Leon's voice had taken on a much more demanding, authoritative tone that left Cassius rather surprised. In all the years he'd known Leon, he had never truly known the man to yell or command anyone.

Not even Eden...

"But Leon—"

"I said, leave us." Leon turned, flashing a dark look at Cora. Cassius noted her eyes looked as if she were on the verge of tears, and she actually had the audacity to stomp her foot like a petulant child in frustration before storming out of the entryway to God knows where.

Leon picked up Cassius's suitcase and motioned for him to follow.

"Come, we have much to catch up on," Leon said as he headed to the opposite side of the house with Cassius's luggage held hostage.

CHAPTER THIRTEEN

AVA STIRRED IN the dead of night, her eyes fluttering as they tried to adjust to the darkness. The heavy hotel blanket fell from her instantly, the chilly air hitting her skin, causing a shiver to race down her spine. She wiped her eyes and let out a groan as her head throbbed.

A quick glance to her left and the

events of the night came crawling back as her gaze fixated on a shirtless Sam Kingsley who clung to his pillow, dead to the world.

Ava's gaze trailed over his exposed torso, and she swiftly lifted the covers only a fraction, just enough to see if she was really dreaming or if she'd lost her marbles completely.

Her cheeks heated at the sight, as reality set in, as the memory came flooding back to her.

The memory of Sam's heated kiss, of the dizzying feeling she'd felt in his presence, likely from her alcohol consumption. Although, she was still quite puzzled about that. Ava was no stranger to drinking, and it usually took far more than three shots of whiskey to do her in.

Perhaps, it was the heat of the moment, perhaps, it was the shots, perhaps, it was the fact that he was Sam-freaking-Kingsley, and he was attractive, famous, and her number one celebrity crush.

He was also extremely knowledgeable and well versed in all the things Ava knew now to be true. Though he was a demonologist first, in the last year or so he'd been building up interest in his to be released *Unbound: Vampires in History & Among Us* documentary, something she had wanted to ask him about but refrained from after his admission that was more than the things he hunted, the things he spoke about on television.

Ava dropped the sheet once more, her senses coming back to her slowly. Aside from her splitting headache, she felt a stinging pain along her inner thighs, where her scars lay.

The memory of how she'd gotten such scars always made her feel uneasy, but she was not embarrassed by them by any means. They were a reminder of her survival, the moment her entire life changed.

The vampire who'd carved through her flesh like butter, leaving her to bleed out had since met his demise, by her hand no less, but it seemed more often than not, the few men who'd actually seen the scars since she obtained them were more than put off by them. They found such scars unsightly, unflattering, and as one brutish asshole had stated, *a turn off.*

But Sam did not seem to mind one

bit, as the memory of his teeth nipping at the flesh they covered caused Ava to flush once more. It hadn't hurt at the time, but now in the dead of night after the fact, they did.

Ava closed her eyes, recalling how Sam had run his tongue over them, causing goosebumps to form on her flesh before diving in to taste her.

Remembered how he'd devoured her like she was his last meal.

And as if such a thing were a curse in itself, the memory of her pleasure melted into memory of the *most* blissful feeling she'd ever felt. Ava's mind wandered to the very thing she'd undoubtedly been trying to forget, the thing she could not seem to escape.

Bliss...

Cassius.

Her mind instead wandered to a wet, warm tongue on her wrist, sealing her wounds with venom, to the blissful feeling of fangs piercing her skin, the rush of blood to the surface.

Even the memory made her heart race, her blood heat, and her thighs clench, As if Cassius were not merely a figment of memory in her brain, but as if he were lying next to her instead of the delicious demonologist who was rather skilled with his tongue.

And in the dark, with her eyes closed... she could pretend he was.

Such a desire caused shame, guilt, and anger to overcome her, as it always did, but Ava did not have time to wallow in her qualms about the sexy vampire who she'd left in Chester, far away from Oklahoma—far away from Sam

Kingsley's hotel room.

A scream startled her out of her fantasies, bringing her back to the here and now. Ava sat up straighter, flinging the covers away as she all but leapt out of the bed.

She hurriedly felt around on the floor for her clothing, dressing as quickly as she could, nearly tripping over her stake, which had fallen out of her boot from the haphazard, clothes-tearing session.

Fuck, I hope Sam didn't notice that...

Another scream, and Ava was out the door in a flash, never looking back as she followed the sound of terror like a moth to a flame.

CHAPTER FOURTEEN

THE MOONLIGHT CAST an ethereal glow on Leon's expansive backyard, turning the grass a shade of deep blue. The trees on the edge of his property loomed over with their full, leafy bounty bristling in the wind. Cassius thought it was a rather beautiful sight, even if it reminded him of *her*.

Eden.

"Why do you insist on running?"
Cassius asked as he hunched over, his
hands braced upon his knees, catching
his breath.

"Ah, yes, well, this is what happens
when one no longer needs to hunt for
their food. You become fat and lazy,"
Eden taunted him.

"I will have you know I am in top
shape, my dear."

"Your undead lungs say otherwise,"
she said with a laugh.

Cassius looked up at her, his gaze
much more haunting than it should have
been, given the light of the full moon on
this night.

The sounds of smooth jazz filled the
air, faint like a ghost. They were far from
the party at hand, and a part of Cassius

longed to go back.

To where it was safe, to where it was warm.

"Perhaps, if you stay in one place, Edie, for more than five seconds you will see just how lively I can be."

Eden turned to him, her ruby red lips curving into a sinful smile he knew all too well.

"Perhaps, I like to be chased, darling. Perhaps, I like the thrill of the hunt."

The moonlight shone on her fair skin, making her bright sapphire blue eyes glow in its wake.

Cassius stood tall, finally catching his breath as she stalked over to him slowly. When she stood only inches away from him, her jeweled eyes caught his with interest. She reached out slowly, pushing a lock of golden hair behind his ear.

"Forgive me, Eden, but I always thought you more of a hunter than prey," *he said darkly, feeling the effects of his champagne, the chill of the wind, and the stirrings of desire in the pit of his stomach.*

"Perhaps, for once, Cassius, I want to be captured," *she whispered against his lips, and Cassius did not wait as he obeyed her and captured her lips with his.*

Leon motioned for Cassius to take a seat, and he did so. It seemed that despite his looks, not much about Leon had changed. Including his hospitable demeanor, as he tried to make Cassius as comfortable as possible. He'd been living with Tajiri and Jasmine for nearly thirty some years and among the three of them, Cassius was the one who took care of most things regarding their abode, and it felt good to be waited on, for once.

"I was not certain I'd ever see you again, Cassius, after our last meeting," Leon said softly.

The memory of their last meeting would never truly fade away, no matter how many years went by.

The rush, the urgency.

Cassius could still feel it as if it were no time at all, even though it had been thirty-five years.

"Cassius, sit down. Please. We can talk about this—"

"There is nothing to talk about, Leon. I am leaving this god-forsaken hellhole and I am never coming back..." Cassius bit as he brushed past Leon with his suitcase.

"You are being irrational right now

because you are angry, and rightfully so. Eden has that effect on many people."

"She killed him, Leon! She killed my father—"

"Cassius..."

Cassius could feel the tears forming in his eyes, and his heart felt as if it were in his throat at the words, the reality of them hitting him like a bag of heavy bricks.

"Because he found out the truth. The child—" Cassius's throat tightened, a mixture of grief, anger, and frustration coursed through him.

He should have known better. It wasn't the first time Eden had kept the truth hidden from him, and he felt a fool for abandoning such notions that she could change, that she was different.

That she loved him.

She'd never loved him. She'd only loved Marcellus Medici. He'd kept her secret, stood by her in her darkest hour. Yet, she'd fought to preserve her own name, preserve her ranking. Had the covens discovered the truth, that Eden and Marcellus had been carrying on an affair, that their affair had resulted in an illegitimate heir—despite the fact that that she'd lost both her lover and her child—

The covens would surely bring her to justice for her actions. After all, she was bonded to the vampire, and that evidence was as solid as the earth beneath his feet. The treaty between the covens would fall into ruin, and it would be war. There would be no trial.

His father, Lucius, posed a threat to her existence, and she killed him so she could live another day. So she could kill, lie, and chase the ghosts that haunted her until there was no magic left to dull the pain.

The worst part was Cassius understood her reasons, but it didn't make any of it right, and it left a sour taste in his mouth.

He could not trust her.

Not now.

Not ever.

And she'd had the audacity to threaten him. As if she could command him like some obedient dog, as if she could make him see he was the irrational one. Her words filtered through his brain, the memory of her expression as her eyes filled with tears.

"So help the gods, Cassius, if you walk out the door..." Her voice shook with fury, with anger. "I will not give you the choice next time. You will obey me," she growled.

"There is always a choice. The fact you fail to understand that, is why I will never be yours to command. You cannot control me, Eden."

Darkness swelled in Cassius's vision as he closed his eyes, trying to fight the hunger inside of him that begged for blood, for release.

A body to sate his turmoil; to quiet the monster inside. What had Eden turned him into?

"I need to leave," he said, his voice echoing in the cavernous room.

***

Cassius brushed his fingers along the glass, feeling the cool water against his skin, pulling him from his painful *thoughts.*

"What about your mother?" Leon pressed, following Cassius as he hurriedly ran down the steps. The way Leon spoke made Cassius stop dead in his tracks, his shoes squeaking on the freshly waxed floor. He turned on his heel, taking a look at Leon before he answered, stilling his breath.

"That is why I came here, to see you. To tell you what I must do. I need you to make sure she is safe, that neither my mother nor Eden will come looking for me."

"You can't be serious," Leon sighed.

"I am. I do not belong here, Leon. I never have. I was not made to be a pawn in some grand scheme erected by the Boracellis, or to be some stud for breeding. I was not meant to love... I—"

"Cassius, you are hurting. It is natural to feel this way, it does not mean—"

"How can you defend her? After all the pain she's caused you?" Cassius felt enraged as Leon's words settled on his ears.

"I am not defending her. I am merely concerned that you are too emotional, right now, and you are not thinking straight."

"I need to be as far away from Eden Boracelli and the god-forsaken High Covens as I can get. I'm done playing their games, Leon. This ends with me."

"And where will you go?" Leon's eyes took on a glassy shimmer of their own as he stood in the foyer, his hands at his side.

Cassius could see the pain in his eyes, and his heart sank.

He'd miss him the most.

"Yes, well, I was rather... what did you say? *Emotional?*"

Leon smirked. "Yes, I think that was the word."

"Not one of my finer moments," Cassius said with a raise of his eyebrow.

"You were in pain, Cassius."

"I was. I was damn heartbroken. Everything I thought was real... it wasn't. And Eden...

"I just couldn't stand to look at her anymore. She'd fallen further into darkness and knowing the truth, about what she did to my father and *why* she did it, knowing that Marcellus was the reason for her madness..." Cassius sighed deeply as he sat back in his chair.

"But I am not here to talk about

Eden. That is ancient history."

"She is still alive, you know."

"I know."

"Really?" Leon said with a raised eyebrow of his own.

"The cabin I reside in, in Virginia, is on the border of Boracelli territory."

"Is that so?"

"A wise man once told me to keep my friends close and my enemies closer. And that is what I do. I keep a low profile, I get by. I stay under the radar. Octavius and his lackeys are too focused on expanding their territory. I don't anticipate them coming back until—"

Cassius shifted in his seat, feeling his throat tighten once more. He wanted to say the words, wanted to tell Leon about Ava. About claiming her. If anyone knew about blood bonds, it would be Leon.

The man was a wealth of knowledge and had never steered Cassius wrong before, but Cassius could also feel a strange protectiveness at even the thought. Though he trusted Leon more than anyone, he felt a strange possessiveness to keep her all to himself. The world had taken much from him, but in its wake, he had found her.

He looked down to his wrist, and for a moment he could have sworn he felt the faint thrum of a pulse in his veins; like a ghost, it slipped away just as soon as it had made its presence known.

"It doesn't matter. All that matters is that you apparently need some guidance of your own," Cassius said with a smirk.

Leon rolled his eyes.

"Cora has always had a flair for the dramatic. I assure you I am fine. She is just blowing things out of proportion."

"Tell me about the deaths."

"The local law enforcement has been trying to pinch me for years because of the club, but I can assure you I run a legitimate establishment."

"Club?" Cassius asked curiously.

"The Dark Hearts Club. To the humans, it is just an average club, nothing more to see than strippers and adult entertainers, but it is built for our kind, it is—"

"A blood den."

"Yes. I've been conducting my research there for the last thirty years. Studying the link, the attraction and sustainable relationship between mortals and vampires."

Cassius felt his blood run cold, and the faint buzzing danced in his veins again. He shook his head, trying to dispel the tricks of his mind. After all, Oklahoma was a large state. But something about Leon's words hit him hard in the chest.

Sustainable relationship.

Cassius had known about Leon's academic undertakings. He'd been studying their biology for centuries at this point. The thought that perhaps he'd uncovered something about the *link* between his kind and the mortals, perhaps could be of use to him somehow, someway... Thoughts of Ava flooded his brain as the flutter of a pulse caused his heart to race.

You're just working yourself up.

You need to relax...

"Cora believes someone is trying to frame you. An investor or someone interested in the club."

"I think she watches too much television."

"Is it possible, though?" Cassius asked.

"The recent string of murders indicates something that is not of our kind. Though the killer has gone through a great deal of trouble to try and present the bodies as vampire victims, which means they are familiar with our kind."

"What do you mean not of our kind?"

"I cannot be certain as I don't have enough evidence, yet. If I could get my hands on the toxicology reports, I would be able to corroborate my theory—"

"English, Leon."

"I believe the one responsible for the murders is not a mortal, or a vampire. I believe, and it is just a hunch at this point…"

"What? What is it?" Cassius felt on the edge of his seat.

Leon looked back at him with a cold expression.

"I believe it is an Incubus. It's been nearly a hundred years since one was seen in these parts, but the details are similar…"

"An Incubus? A sex demon?" Cassius raised his eyebrow. He'd been fortunate enough to evade demons, save for a brief time in the '20s… but even then, the demons he'd known then were run of the mill crossroad demons, save for a few Succubi. He'd never come into contact with an Incubus before.

"As I said, I cannot confirm or deny my theory without substantial evidentiary findings."

"Perhaps I can help with that," Cassius said, feeling bold. "I am quite the professional when it comes to morgues," he said seriously.

Leon only smiled. "Perhaps you can."

CHAPTER FIFTEEN

THE BRIGHT FLUORESCENT lights buzzed loudly in the hallway, their vivid light only adding to the pounding in Ava's head. She brought her arm up to shield herself from the light for a moment, adjusting to her surroundings. The deafening sound of a thud sounded to her right, and without thinking Ava turned to follow.

The hallway loomed in front of her like some carpeted labyrinth, twisting and turning until the sounds of struggle, of wet sucking became louder. With her stake poised in her hands, Ava leaned against the wall, keeping as quiet as possible. The scar on her wrist heated, and she could feel an energy in the air that was most profound.

Thrall.

Ava knew without a doubt the vampire was near, and she took a moment to catch her breath.

As she turned the corner, stake at the ready, her eyes widened in surprise. The vampire turned, eyes glowing with anger. The short red-haired woman had her claws wrapped up in Vinny's jacket, and Ava could see he was struggling to fight off the young woman who looked like she couldn't be a day over sixteen.

"Let him go," Ava said as she rushed toward the vampire.

The woman reared her teeth in defense, a deep hiss escaping her throat.

Ava moved to push the vampire off but was not so lucky.

The vampire let Vinny go, but within moments her long nails were wrapped around Ava's neck, and her blue eyes were filled with rage.

Vinny slid down to the ground, coughing, trying to regain his breath.

"Ava... what the..."

Ava wrapped her hand around the vampire's wrist with all her might.

The red headed vampire focused her angry gaze on Ava like a hypnotizing snake.

Lust started to form in Ava's belly, her head started to feel foggy.

The telltale effect of thrall hard at work, vying to make her pliable to be vampire chow.

The very same images that always accosted her, especially when feeling a vampire's thrall, filtered in through her thoughts without warning. Thoughts of glowing green emeralds, of the warmth of Cassius's mouth on her skin, how it would feel against her throat.

How his fangs would feel deep inside her flesh.

Ava could not help the moan of ecstasy that escaped her throat as the vampire *giggled*.

She'd been in this exact position quite a few times, and thanks to Mal and Dallas's training, she was more than well versed in how to combat the vampire's Jedi mind tricks.

Ava fought against the thoughts, battling them with memories of her own; vicious ones that would forever be rooted within her, would haunt her nightmares forever.

The memory of her parents' bodies, cold in a puddle of blood on the living room floor.

Of Ross, her college boyfriend, his life drained from him, discarded like a shell in the corner.

Of the vampire's sneer as he plunged the knife in her skin; of the pain.

Ava leaned forward, bringing her heavy hand up, fingers grasped around the stake.

A groaning Vinny moved to stand, but a loud banging sound distracted them all, and before Ava knew it, the vampire headbutted her.

"The fuck!" Ava said as she dropped her stake, her hands moving to her head, which was throbbing now more than ever.

Ava stumbled, falling to the floor, her vision blurred.

Out of her peripheral vision, she watched the vampire disappear into the shadows of the stairwell.

"Fuck, Ava... Are you okay?" Vinny said as he moved in front of her.

"Did she bite you?" Ava asked as she squinted her eyes shut, the light more intrusive now than when she'd awakened.

"No, I'm not bit... but... there was a girl... in the stairwell... I—"

"Fucking hell..." Ava groaned.

Vinny's hands softly wrapped around Ava's wrists, and the touch made her jump. His hands on her skin were rough to the touch, but he pulled at her hands gently.

"Let me take a look" His breath was hot on her skin, and he smelled vaguely of cigarettes and whiskey.

"I'm fine, I—" But Ava did not have the will to fight him, and she was suddenly very tired.

"Stay with me, Ava," Vinny said, his voice slightly panicked.

"I'm tired..." Ava said as his hands settled her own in her lap. He brushed his thumb against her eyebrow, the motion bringing him closer to her.

"Shit Ava, you're bleeding pretty bad. Probably going to need some stitches." His voice vibrated on her skin, and she could feel slumber beckoning her.

"Nothing a good sleep can't fix," she whispered.

Vinny wrapped his arms around her, and she felt him pull her up. He placed her arm around his back, his arms holding her at his waist.

"In a little bit. First things first, we gotta get you cleaned up, okay?" His voice was soft, even.

It reminded her of Cassius.

Ava could hear the clicking of the lock, the electronic whirr that told her the door was ready to open. Vinny held her closer as he entered the doorway, his arms tight around her. Ava brushed against his chest, breathing in his smokey scent.

It smelled like Mal.

Like home.

"What the hell, Vinny? What happened?" A dark voice broke the silence.

"Where's Mal?" Vinny asked as he maneuvered them over to a bed.

Ava fell onto it instantly, wanting to curl up on the pillows.

"No, no, no sleep yet," Vinny soothed her.

Ava groaned.

"Fuck if I know. Do I look like his mother to you?" the voice bit.

Ava knew that sarcasm, that bite anywhere.

Dallas.

"Well, considering we were just attacked by a fucking vamp, I'd be a little more concerned."

"He said he was meeting up with someone," Dallas said as he lifted Ava up, pulling her into his lap. A part of her felt angered by the motion, but another part felt a satisfying warmth as he held her up while Vinny moved about gathering supplies. She could not help as she sunk back against him, closing her eyes. She took a deep breath, focusing on the sounds of the hunters' voices.

"Well, for the moment that's probably a good thing," Vinny said.

"Did you get a good luck at the bloodsucker?" Dallas asked, his hands tight on Ava's arms, and she could almost feel a tremble in them.

Then again, it was probably the mixture of a hangover and a rattle to the brain.

Because nothing made Jake Dallas tremble.

The man was built from steel.

"Yeah, you could say that. Got pretty up close and personal," Vinny answered definitively.

"I saved his ass," Ava said, flashing a smile.

"Damn right you did," Vinny's warm voice sounded close to her face, and she could feel his rough fingers on her temple, touching a spot on her head that stung. A cold liquid mixed in with the blood, with her flesh, the sting somehow worse than only moments ago.

"Fuck... that stings."

Dallas's hand slid down her arm, resting just above hers, his thumb brushing her knuckle.

"I know, I'm sorry. I'll try to be quick, here," Vinny said as she felt a pinch through her skin, and the pain heightened.

"Christ!" Ava lurched forward. "Aren't you supposed to like, warn me? Give me an anesthetic or some shit?" Ava grumbled.

Vinny ignored her, focusing on his tight stitching.

Dallas grabbed her hand and squeezed.

"Squeeze if it hurts, okay? That way Vinny gets to live another day," Dallas whispered in her ear just as another stitch went through.

Ava squeezed his hand tightly, so tightly she thought her own fingers may break.

"Good girl," Dallas whispered, his breath hot against her neck, his voice dark and somehow relaxing.

The tone, how faint it sounded, Ava

knew only she could hear him. She was not sure how to feel about that, not sure how to comprehend anything except the innate desire to fall into Dallas or Vinny or whoever's bed it was she was camped out on.

"Okay, that just about does it," Vinny said as he cut the last piece of thread and Ava felt all the tension, all the exhaustion as the evening's events caught up to her.

"Can I go to sleep now?" she murmured.

"Yeah, you can go to sleep. We'll take turns taking watch," Dallas said matter-of-factly.

"Watch?" Ava said as she pushed out of Dallas's hold, curling up on the unmade bed, pulling herself against a pillow that smelled vaguely spicy, like smoke and cinnamon.

It wasn't a terrible scent, and she breathed it in, letting it fill her lungs.

"Well, I mean you were hit in the head. Probably should just keep an eye on you to make sure you don't have a concussion," Vinny said as he put away the needle, thread, and alcohol.

"Don't tell my brother," Ava grumbled.

"Wouldn't dream of it, Kitten," Dallas said as he ran his hand up and down her back, the motion lulling her into a well-deserved sleep.

CHAPTER SIXTEEN

CASSIUS WALKED ALONG Ansley's Main Street, taking in the sight of the bars and shops, the businesses that littered the sides of the street. Like Chester, it was positively perfect in design, right down to the shiny mailboxes that were without graffiti or marking.

The last time he'd been on Main Street, it had looked quite different. In fact, it was a different time altogether. Where the White Barn Candle shop lay, Cassius could still see fresh in his mind the café that existed there once upon a time in the days after Prohibition. The ornate bronze trim molding still existed around the exterior, reminding him of the shimmer it had in the moonlight of long ago.

When he'd been a different man.

A man who thought he'd found love but was sorely deceived. What existed between Eden and him was not love. It was lust, half-truths, and lies. It was fabricated, arranged by those who knew nothing of love.

Not really.

Though it was late, the streets were

fairly empty. The neon lights of the bars cast hazy pink, purple, and blue shadows on the cobblestone street, reflecting in the puddles in the cracks in the sidewalk, a most relaxing sight. When he finally found himself in front of The Dark Hearts Club, he stopped to take in the sight.

Cassius had been to a few blood dens back in his early years as a newborn, that first time being the night he'd agreed to venture out with Marcellus Medici and his friends, with Octavius, Eden's brother. His friend.

At least, at the time Octavius was not a foe. In fact, he was the closest thing Cassius had to a best friend. Someone in his corner, no matter what.

He'd never cared much for the blood dens, feeling a strange sense of protectiveness over the men and women who chose a life of servitude to their *immortal gods*.

Many entered the ring of servitude willingly, but there were those who simply had no other option.

It's no different than a whorehouse, Cassius.

Octavius's words still made his stomach twist several centuries later, what with the way he'd carelessly spoke them, Cassius should have known his value for life was more in line with his sister's than either of them would have liked to acknowledge.

The outside of The Dark Hearts Club was lit by the same pink, blue, and purple neon glow that seemed prevalent on all the bars on this street, but the shimmering black obsidian pillars, the sleek glass...

It was all very modern, sensual even. Cassius's stomach growled once more, his mouth watering at the prospect that lay behind the walls of the club.

Leon's club.

Cora had claimed Leon was being blackmailed, that someone was out to frame Leon to try and gain the upper hand, gain access to the club.

To cut him out of the equation completely.

But why?

Cassius knew his answers lay on the other side of the door. Though the nerves flooded his body, his wrist flaring with heat as his blood warmed, and thoughts of fresh, warm blood pushed forth.

It wasn't just the thought of blood

that persisted in his memory like a record on repeat.

Oh no.

It was the thought of his fangs piercing soft, pale flesh, of his fingers brushing away silken chocolate locks, trailing his fingertips along her skin.

Ava's skin, in particular.

The woman he'd *claimed*.

It was the fantasy of tasting her blood, letting it run down his throat, letting it fill him to the brim until he was so sated on it there'd only be one way to calm the fever that fresh blood brings.

Cassius swallowed nervously, sliding his hands in his pockets.

I can do this.

It's just a little recognizance.

I'm just getting a lay of the land, just checking things out.

I am stronger than my instincts.

Though as he thought the words, he knew it was more than that. He chose to believe the lie instead, as he pulled open the heavy glass doors and headed into The Dark Hearts Club.

The inside was just as cool in color and temperature as the outside and didn't look all that different from the average strip club.

Cassius had done his fair share of gallivanting with Tajiri in the years since he'd shown up in Chester, if only because he enjoyed the company of the man rather than the thrill of hunting. After all, he didn't hunt anymore, but he'd always enjoyed being a part of the world, even as a wallflower keenly observing life as it went on in his midst.

Though the world may have changed

around him, some things remained constant forever. Parties, sex, alcohol; the high of youthfully being free... of living in the moment... Those things never grew old for humanity.

Cassius casually stalked over toward the bar, taking in the sight of the club and its inhabitants before him like a cheetah observing its prey. He'd forgone such vicious things as hunting, as feasting on the living—there were always blood dens like The Dark Hearts Club throughout the years, which made feeding much more streamlined, but Cassius never felt right about it, not after what had happened to Marguerite... The only woman he'd ever fed off of, even if it was only a brief time.

Instead, he traded such things in for a steady supply of corpse blood from the local morgue. Before long, he'd have to make the trip, if the dryness in his throat and mouth was any indication.

His gaze scoured over a dancer on the main stage, teetering on her Lucite heels, wearing some sort of black vinyl contraption that strategically covered just enough of her pale flesh to be considered a bikini. He watched, frozen in his tracks as her crystalline-blue eyes caught him, watched as she ran her hands up from her navel, squeezing her breasts softly before sliding them around her throat. She rolled her head back, long, dark hair cascading over her shoulders, lit up in the blue neon. The sight stirred a mixture of emotion in him, of desire and memories long forgotten.

Memories of *her.*

The wicked queen.

Eden.

His fangs *ached* for the blood coursing beneath the dancer's neck, which her fingers traced over suggestively. Her tongue graced her pouty lips just before she took the flesh in between her teeth, and Cassius forced himself to break her gaze.

I do not have time for this.

This is not what I came here for.

He moved to the back of the room quietly, observing the foxes and the vixens of the den. And as he hid in the corners, watching life as it lived right before his eyes, he noticed a familiar head of red hair turning the corner, looking around panic-stricken before a man stepped up and blocked his view.

Cora looked around the man once

more, her eyebrows knitting together in slight worry before they too disappeared into the shadows, into the crowd.

Cassius sidled up to the bar, which wasn't looking overly populated, at the moment. In fact, there were only a few club goers spread out between the barstools. The same pink, blue, and purple neon lit up the back of the bar and all the frosted liquor glasses, and Cassius noted the large smoked glass mirror that stretched the length of the bar. He could see his reflection, illuminated by the neon glow.

He'd been in several blood dens over the years, but this one was the first since he'd gone off fresh blood completely.

Though the times had changed, he knew the structure would not, and without a doubt the real attraction was below deck, and likely, one needed special access to attend the actual dens in which feedings took place. Which is why the upper level was so important. Something needed to distract the humans so they would not be the wiser to what was really going on. The smoke and mirrors were a part of life for a vampire. One needed to blend in seamlessly into the background, into the fabric of life in order to live another day, undetected.

"Slow night?" Cassius asked nonchalantly as the bartender came to his end of the bar. The man was quite stocky, the sides of his head shaved, while a sleek, generous coif of hair was gelled into a perfect shape on top of his head. His strategically cut and lined facial hair only added to the brooding look this man had about him, and he leaned against the bar, swishing around a toothpick in his mouth.

Behind him, Cassius could hear the music changing, signaling the next stripper to take the stage. The melody of some man crooning about "preying on you tonight" and hunting one down to eat them alive filled the air.

"No, actually, I'm kind of glad there's a break. Must be a big event or something over at the Starling. This place has been packed nonstop since that fucking convention rolled in. Not that I'm complaining, though," the bartender said as he dragged a clean rag up and down the sleek black marble bar.

The neon, the marble... even the mirror.

Everything about the place felt familiar to Cassius, and when the first notes of "Cherry Pie" by Warrant started to play, Cassius couldn't help the smile that formed across his face.

Memories of the first time he'd met Taj, in a club in the mid-eighties, pushed forth and Cassius had to appreciate the finer details. But, unfortunately, he was not here to appreciate the ambiance.

No.

He'd spent nearly all his life in and out of bars, clubs, and cafés, so he knew better than anyone the best source for information on the town happenings was the man who poured the drinks. The anonymous ear of a bartender was worth its weight in gold.

"What can I get you?" the bartender

asked as he swished his toothpick around in his mouth again.

Cassius eyed the lit expanse of bottles, noting the labels were top shelf. Leon always did prefer the finer things in life.

"What is the oldest wine you have?"

"Oldest? Like shelf life or..."

"Aged," Cassius said.

"Up here, the oldest I got is this Cab." The bartender brought the bottle over to Cassius, who inspected it. The label was not particularly helpful, but it did say the wine was a vintage, bottled during the early nineties. He preferred a well aged Bordeaux, but it would have to do.

"I'll take a glass, please."

"Shit, I never thought I'd see *anyone* else drink this sour cherry shit. Only the owner requests it, which is why we keep it on hand."

"Surely, he won't mind," Cassius said with a smirk.

"I won't tell, if you don't," the bartender said with a smile as he poured the wine.

"Thank you," Cassius said as he swirled it around, letting the aromatic notes fill his airways. He took a deep breath before taking a sip.

Sour my ass.

"Ah. Delicious. Your owner has good taste."

"He thinks he does, anyway." The bartender chuckled. "I'd rather get shitfaced on a good scotch than over some stuffy old wine, but what do I know. I just work here."

Cassius figured it was now or never and decided to go for the kill.

"Have you heard anything about that case… the… murder at the Silver Starling? They ever find the guy who did it?" Cassius said as he leaned casually on the bumper rail of the bar, looking nonplussed. He took extra attention to speak casually, eradicating the refined touch of enunciation he'd garnered throughout the years. Though it wasn't something he utilized frequently, he could make himself sound modern, natural. Like any other twenty-four-year-old.

"Actually, they tried arresting my boss for it, which is crazy. He might be an eccentric dude, but he ain't a killer."

"Eccentric?" Cassius couldn't help the smile that formed on his lips.

Well, that's one way to describe Leon.

"Yeah. Lives in this old creepy house,

keeps to himself, mostly. Aside from his weekly visits here, that is. I swear he's either perpetually single or gay, even though he hangs out with this smoking redhead." The bartender whistled.

Cassius took another sip of his wine.

"How does one get access to the dens downstairs?" Cassius said as if he was asking for the weather.

The bartender's smile faded, replaced by an unreadable, impenetrable one.

"How do you know—"

"Your owner is a friend," Cassius answered softly, and the bartender pursed his lips. When Cassius had thought his venture had failed, the man spoke.

"What kind of friend?"

Cassius felt a relief come over him and he sipped his wine once more, draining the last bit. The liquid came too quickly, and some of it dribbled down his chin. He casually wiped it away with his thumb before speaking.

"Why, only the best kind," he said with a smile, exposing just the tip of his fang.

"Unfortunately, we close in an hour, so... the den is booked for the remainder of the evening."

"I can make a reservation?"

"You can come when the club opens and speak with Louie. He's in charge of the basement, and... payment, of course."

Cassius slid his hand into his pockets pulling out his wallet.

"Thank you," he said as he counted out a small stack of bills that were probably too much for the sole drink, but he did not think twice about leaving a large tip.

The man had been more than agreeable to answering his questions. As Cassius turned on his heel, readying for his exit, his gaze settled on the stage once more. The woman on the stage looked familiar with her lithe, pale frame dangling from the pole, only held up by the crook of her knee latching on for dear life. She pulled herself around the pole slowly, angling to get a look at the crowd before flexing her leg straight up the side of the pole as if she had no bones in her legs at all.

Cassius watched as she pushed away once more, feigning disinterest as she tried to escape the confines of the neon light of the stage.

When she turned to face the audience

on her left, toward him, his heart stopped.

Crystalline-blue eyes stared back at him once more, long, straight red hair falling over her pale shoulders down to her waist, the swell of her pert, round breasts straining against her tight blue, triangle bikini top that looked like it was barely held together by string.

"Like what you see?" The bartender jabbed him with a chuckle.

"I, uh... need to go," Cassius said as he turned away, sliding into the shadows and away from Cora's line of sight.

CHAPTER SEVENTEEN

THE BLOOD WAS everywhere. Saturated in the threads of the carpet, streaked against the floral wallpaper. The bodies, lifeless in the corner, discarded like trash. The eyes of her parents, once so full of life were now nothing but soulless voids.

Ava reached out across the space between, but it was too distant. There was nothing she could do. Nothing could bring them back. Nothing could turn back time.

Her vision was blurry, mascara streaking down her cheeks like black oiled tears. She wiped them away, smearing the makeup all along her cheeks. She saw what she'd missed all those years ago.

The puncture marks in her father's neck, all along her mother's wrists and forearm.

And the world turned to dust and debris once more, the wallpaper dissolving into the dark, dank walls of a frat house basement, and Ava was no longer reaching for her parents.

She held her hand out in the darkness, and something reached back.

Warm, soft fingers stroked her wrist,

grasping around her, pulling her closer.

How desperately she wanted to follow, wanted to rise from the depths of the puddle of blood, and fall into the arms of her savior.

But when she looked into the eyes of her hero, she knew he was no savior.

For the fangs he bore and the blood that stained his porcelain skin would never go away. No, this gallant angel of death who had saved her life was not a hero.

He was a monster.

He killed people, people like her parents. Like the monsters who had killed Ross, who had left her alone to die. But he'd spared her, for some reason...

Ava rose from the puddle of blood, which had turned from blood to ash. The embers surrounded her like the dust and leaves around her ankles on a mid-evening walk in Chester in the fall.

Ava let Cassius pull her close. Close enough he could wrap his arms around her waist, close enough she could run her hands up his heathered-gray shirt and feel the solid expanse of his chest beneath her fingertips. Close enough that his breath on her skin could elicit goosebumps and make her blood boil like a witch's cauldron on Halloween.

"What are you waiting for?" he whispered, his voice sultry and smooth in the dead of night like some beautiful lullaby.

Ava blinked, looking around, trying to fight the fog that had settled in her brain, and all around them.

They stood in the open, underneath the moon, where she was acutely aware *they were indeed alone. No one would find them here.*

Not Mal, or the hunters.

Not Dallas.

Certainly not Dallas.

No, in the corners of her subconscious, they were truly alone. She leaned into him, gazing up at him through her long lashes into his emerald-green irises. The shadows fell across his angelic face, the blood from his fangs dripping down his chin almost black in the light.

It would be so easy to just... give in. To let herself submit to the salvation, the promise she knew her stake would bring.

She could stake him easily, like this. He wouldn't even blink, this close, entranced by her blood.

By her mark.

His mark.

It would be so easy to just... end it all. Kill him, as she knew she should. There was no proof it would take away the mark, but... perhaps, it was the only way. Every other option Mal had come across hadn't worked, and it was a long shot...

Cassius's fingers trailed over the scar on her wrist softly as he brought his lips to her ear, his hair brushing against her temple.

"I don't..." Ava swallowed harshly, trying to find the words, trying to fight the maddening feeling radiating all throughout her body, the haziness of her thoughts, her racing heartbeat.

The building warmth and moisture between her legs.

It didn't feel like thrall, but what else could it be?

"I don't know," she whispered back as her fingers ran up his neck, finding their way into his hair, tugging on the locks tightly.

Cassius embraced her, his hold tightening like a vice.

"Oh, my sweet Avarice. I think you do. Perhaps, you need to stop fighting, stop running... for there are monsters out there..."

Cassius's lips brushed the skin of her neck softly, suckling at her flesh, his warm tongue causing butterflies in her stomach and a most pleasant wetness that spread like wildfire in between her thighs.

"Monsters I can't save you from," Cassius whispered, his voice vibrating on her skin, dark like the shadows that pulled him from her grasp into the

darkness once more...

Ava shifted into a hard, warm mass as the edges of her dream started to fall away. The warm mass smelled good, felt rather cozy and comfortable, and she burrowed her face into it once more.

"Well, good morning to you, too," a gruff, gravelly, sleep-tinged voice settled on her ears and, for a moment, it sounded just as comfortable as she felt snuggled against...

Dallas.

Ava's immediately opened her eyes and shot up to confirm she wasn't still dreaming.

No.

Her gaze settled on Dallas, on his deep blue eyes, his five o'clock shadow. On that chiseled jaw, thick arms, and...

She pushed herself away from Dallas

and nearly jumped off the bed, but the motion was too much and she felt dizzy.

Dallas wrapped his hand around her wrist and tugged, causing her to fall back into the messy covers.

"Rule number one when dealing with Hunter Triage..." he grumbled as she groaned.

"There are rules, now?"

Dallas let out a chuckle.

"There have always been rules, Kitten. You and your brother just don't seem to think they apply to you."

"Well, that's because they don't," she said with a huff as she moved to get up.

Dallas's grip tightened.

"Rule number one," Dallas continued as if she hadn't even spoken.

"No man gets left behind. We take care of our fellow hunters. Always."

Something in the way he said the words made Ava feel panicked. Why, she could not be certain. It wasn't as if it was a terrible rule. To watch out for one another, make sure your other hunters were taken care of if injured. But something about his words, the tone of his voice... it was as if he was saying something else.

Something she did not want to hear.

Not now.

"Let me go, Dallas," she said, turning her head and casting him a warning glance.

"What were you doing there last night? Vinny was all the way on the other side of the hotel, and you two weren't patrolling together. I would know."

Ava pursed her lips, and her blood

started to heat at his insinuation.

"What's it to you? You don't fucking own me." She pulled against his grip, but instead of breaking it, she only ended up pulling him closer.

Dallas looked past her, and she turned to follow his glance. Vinny lay sound asleep on top of the covers, soft snores coming from his half open mouth. Dallas's voice was a dark whisper; full of things Ava didn't want to acknowledge at the moment.

I don't have time for this...

"You're right, I don't..." Ava's gaze caught Dallas's, and in them she could see fire.

Anger, jealousy.

But what did Dallas have to be angry about?

It wasn't like they were... anything.

She didn't owe him shit.

"But if you did, you certainly wouldn't have ended up with fucking stitches. I would have made sure you were safe."

Ava pulled with all her might against his grip and broke away. His hand fell to the mattress, and though every bone in her body told her to leave, every siren blaring that this... whatever *this* was between them, was not something she should pursue, she could not help rising to the occasion.

She could never resist having the last word. She couldn't resist a fight, and Jake Dallas made her feel as if every moment was fight or flight.

"Maybe I don't need anyone to keep me safe. Maybe..." She leaned closer, close enough she could stake him.

If he were a vampire, which he was

not.

But from the way Dallas was looking at her, and the slight sting she could still feel from his touch, she was not certain he wasn't some creature sent from the depths of Hell to destroy her and her quest for... vengeance?

Sanity?

Ava wasn't sure.

"Maybe I'm capable of rescuing my own damn self," she said as she got up from Dallas's bed and made her way to the door.

"I believe the words you're looking for are *thank you*," Dallas growled.

Ava stopped in front of the door, turning only to give Dallas a one-finger salute before leaving and slamming the door shut so loud she was certain it would have woken the dead.

***

Ava cursed as she realized upon her arrival to her hotel room, that she'd left her clutch in Sam Kingsley's hotel room. She leaned her head against the door in defeat, the motion stretching her skin only enough to send a twinge of fresh pain through her head.

"Get your shit together, Ava," she mumbled to herself as she pushed off the door, heading for the front desk. A quick glance at the giant grandfather clock in the hall told her the convention's panels and programs likely would have already started, which meant Sam was likely nowhere near his hotel room.

Ava slid her hands in her overall pockets as she sauntered down the corridor, her disheveled hair, smeared makeup, and fresh stitches only adding a more gruesome element to her original Chucky cosplay. In fact, the number of nods, thumbs up, and people who'd stopped her along the way for a picture made her wonder as if she should truly consider splitting skin every time she dressed up in the future, for authenticity's sake.

Upon reaching the lobby, the sunlight streamed through the revolving doors, and it was terribly bright. Bright enough when she tore her vision from it, she could still see spots. She leaned on the cold acrylic countertop, peering down at the concierge.

"May I help you?" he asked drudgingly.

"I lost my keycard. Can I get another

one, please?" she said as politely as possible.

"You were given two."

"Yes, but I lost the one, and the other is locked in my room," she huffed.

When the concierge rolled his eyes, Ava had to bite her tongue. She knew the best way to get what she was asking was to be polite and understanding; every bone in her body wanted to holler and shout a few choice words at the man behind the desk who was testing her sanity.

She was tired, aggravated, and very much in need of a hot shower. Her fate lay in the hands of a concierge who looked like he'd rather be anywhere than the Silver Starling.

So she changed her tactic. She loosened her shoulders, sighing in desperation, feeling her eyes already starting to water.

"I'm sorry to bother you, really, but I just... I don't know what else to do. I..." She even added a fake sniffle for effect as she wiped her eyes.

The concierge's shoulders softened, and his face looked panicked.

"Miss, please, don't cry..."

Bingo.

Perfectly on cue, she let out a rather loud sob, loud enough the people behind her could hear, and the people in the line beside her looked over in worry and disgust at the concierge.

"I'm sorry, I just..."

"What was your room number?" he asked in a low whisper.

Ava had to fight a smile.

"Room 213," she said with another

sniffle.

"Okay, I'm not usually supposed to do this but... please... just... don't cry, okay? We can fix this just... hold on, okay?" he said dejectedly.

"O...okay," she responded.

Within minutes she had a brand new, shiny key card to room 213.

***

Ava had showered long enough the water had gone cold.

But she had a plan. The ghost hunt being led by select members of the cast of *Hell on Earth* she'd hoped to get in on did not start until nine, which meant she had more than enough time to get herself together and enjoy the convention as she'd planned to. That included attending Sam's panel on vampires at noon, where she hoped she could nonchalantly ask about retrieving her clutch.

She towel-dried her hair, glancing at herself in the mirror. The stitches above her eyebrow did make her look slightly menacing, and a part of her wondered if covering them up or camouflaging them with makeup would only irritate her wound. Perhaps, she could just tell her brother it was makeup, anyway. If she even saw him today. They'd planned on going to the vampire panel together, but Dallas had mentioned Mal had gone out and off the radar. Likely, he had a better night than she did, wherever he was waking up, stitches-free.

She slid into a pair of dark wash jeans with more frays and holes than should be classified as pants, and a plain black tank top, tousling her hair for added volume. Sliding the keycard into her back pocket, she opted for just a simple swipe of dark plum lipstick and some black eyeliner.

Her body still ached from exertion, from her rigorous activity of sex and fighting off a bloodsucker—the combination leaving her feeling in desperate need of an Advil and a venti caramel macchiato with at least two shots of espresso.

She kneeled on the ground, fingering through her envelope of cash she'd stashed in a small zip pouch. Everyone on the forums mentioned bringing a Ziplock of cash and only allotting a small amount every day to try and save money. At this moment, she was thankful she'd taken the advice, if only because her clutch with the remaining forty dollars she'd had for yesterday was currently sitting in the room of the man she'd...

Fucked.

The reality hit her in the light of day.

She'd gotten into bed with the host of *Hell on Earth,* and though part of her experience was foggy at best, she remembered it had been rather enjoyable.

The way he'd used his mouth to bring her to the edge.

Or the way he'd kissed her neck, while thrusting deep inside her, his teeth grazing her skin like...

Ava forced the thought down.

No, best not go down that road.

Not like it's going to happen again, anyway...

The moment of forgetting was gone once more, and she closed her eyes, trying to force the thoughts of lips on skin, of fangs in her neck away.

That will never happen, either.

Over my dead body.

***

"What the hell are you doing here?" Ava said in surprise as she came up to the line for Sam's vampire panel.

Dallas slid his hands in his jean pockets, looking bored, while Vinny, Tito, and Hunter seemed to be enjoying their own coffees with smiles on their faces.

"Babysitting," Dallas grumbled.

"Fuck you, you didn't have to come, you know." Hunter jabbed Dallas in the arm.

"And miss this asshole trying to spout off a bunch of lies? Why would I want to miss that?" Dallas drawled sarcastically.

Ava pursed her lips. "What makes you think they're lies?" she asked as she forced her way in line with the hunters, garnering her a few choice looks from others in line.

"Please. Guys like Sam Kingsley are a dime a dozen. They think they know shit because they read some books, watched a few Stephen King movies, but they don't know shit. They're just there to look pretty and boost ratings."

"Have you ever watched *Hell on Earth*?" Ava said, feeling strangely defensive.

"I don't need to watch it. I live it, Kitten."

"Dallas hates TV," Vinny chimed in.

"What are you, an alien?" Ava jabbed as she took a sip of her coffee.

"Ha, ha. Very funny. No, I just don't see the point in wasting my time on shit that isn't real. I have bigger things to worry about than whether or not the stupid ghosts showed up and answered some guy who shouldn't be in their space to begin with."

"Then leave. Why force yourself to do something you don't want to do?"

Before Dallas could answer her, the onslaught of the line lurched forward, and he broke her gaze. Ava followed the crowd into the expansive ballroom, realizing there was one person missing from the equation.

"Where's Mal?" she asked as she squeezed past Dallas to get ahead.

"Probably somewhere better than

here." Dallas winked.

"Gross," Ava said as she wrinkled her nose.

"What?" Vinny asked innocently. "It's not a secret or anything Mal is a bit of a..."

"I do not need to know the sexual practices of my brother, thank you very much, Vinny," Ava said as she grabbed a seat near the front. Dallas sat next to her, while Vinny took the other side, Hunter and Tito finishing up beside him.

The stream of people kept pouring in.

"Whatever, I'm just saying I wouldn't worry about him right now. I'm sure he'll turn up this afternoon somewhere. If he doesn't, then I'd worry."

Just as everyone had gotten settled in their seats, the man in the row in front of them turned and looked at Ava. "Did you hear they found another body?" His eyes sparkled with excitement as he spoke, all too eager to discuss the information.

"No, I didn't. Where..." Ava glanced at Vinny.

"I guess they're trying to keep it hush, since the big fiasco the last time. Startled everyone too much when they came barreling into Sam's last panel."

"Oh really?" Dallas crossed his arms, raising an eyebrow.

"Maybe they just don't have any evidence he did anything. Maybe they're actually looking for the person who—"

Ava's words were cut off when the lights dimmed, the spotlight shining on the stage where the table of speakers lay empty.

Within seconds, the applause was

roaring as the cast of *Hell on Earth* took the stage. Sam and his team of investigators walked out in the spotlight, taking their seats.

Ava couldn't help the way her eyes roved over Sam, over his defined arms, remembering the feeling of his fingers, or the force from his hips. She pressed her legs together, trying to still the sensation building within her, her fingernails digging into her jeans as she held her breath.

Sam's fingers slid over her stomach, down to her aching center and pushed her thighs apart, fitting himself flush against her. Fingers traveling all over, her nerves lit up like a powder keg. His dark voice in her ear, his lips hovering over her throbbing vein in her neck as he urged her to come.

Ava felt the blush sting her cheeks as she tried to force the thoughts down, but looking at Sam in the spotlight, his features more prominent against the contrast of shadows and light, it was all too difficult to fight.

And when he took his seat up front and center on the stage, when he looked out into the crowd and saw her...

He smiled, and suddenly Ava felt flush with heat, her brain slightly foggy again as the desire came back full force, but she pushed against it, knowing she needed to focus. It wasn't like her to come undone over a man so quickly, but then again, Sam Kingsley wasn't just a man. He was a demonologist, a celebrity, and he had been more than a good time. Perhaps, as luck would have it, she was not so unlucky after all. Perhaps, fate had intervened and left her clutch in his hotel room for a reason. Leaving a belonging in someone's house or car was a surefire way to get an invite back. It was one of the oldest tricks in the book, and Ava couldn't help but smile at Sam in return, a most wicked grin of her own, and when he smirked at her, licking his lips slowly, she thought perhaps Sam Kingsley was not meant to be a one night stand after all.

CHAPTER EIGHTEEN

CASSIUS DID NOT *need* to sleep, but sleeping was a difficult habit to break. Especially when given the fact that, from time to time, he did feel tired.

Perhaps the ever-present memories that would not go away in this wretched town were to blame. For every corner he seemed to turn, he was assaulted with bits and pieces of a life he'd lived long ago.

Especially here, in Leon's mansion.

Cassius twisted and turned in his bed, which was much larger and much more comfortable than the one he'd grown accustomed to in the woods of Chester. His bed at home was a solid queen size bed, though big enough for two people, of which Cassius knew no one but him would ever sleep in. Therefore, there was no need for anything larger or fuller.

Taj had been much more favorable to sating the lust that was always present with the hunger for blood and until he'd met Jasmine, their bachelor pad was mostly Taj's bachelor pad.

He'd never judged the man for feeding his desires. Unlike most vampires, Tajiri kept his hunting, feeding, and his desires on a strict schedule. Selecting victims, he'd always chosen individuals he knew would not be missed, or who had no one to question if they'd gone missing. A skill he'd no doubt picked up through the years by patrolling the nearby university and dive bars when the drifters tended to fall.

But in Leon's mansion, in his large guestroom, Cassius found himself surrounded by memory.

Cassius stared into Eden's deep sapphire eyes, and he knew there was no going back from this. On some instinctive level, he knew.

They'd both lost people in this invisible war; the one fought between covens.

She'd lost a man she loved.

She'd lost a child.

There were many who thought Eden was damaged, incapable of such things.

But Cassius knew differently.

Eden Boracelli was not a monster.

She was broken, but wasn't he as well?

Cassius reached out across the space between them, pushing a stray raven hair behind her ear.

He'd always found her to be attractive, from the moment they'd met. But now...

Covered in blood—blood from the hunters who had almost killed him—he was certain he'd never seen anything quite as beautiful.

"Leon will have a fit if he stains the carpet," Cassius whispered.

Eden smiled. "Then perhaps, we should take care of him, now."

But Cassius could not find it within him to move from this space. Not here, not now.

His heart beat steadily, a side effect from the blood they'd consumed.

"There are more pressing matters," he uttered.

Eden slid her arms around his neck and pulled him closer, until her lips brushed his softly. Cassius felt on the edge of a precipice. He wanted to kiss her back. He wanted so much more than to kiss her back.

"Why do you fight this, Cassius?" she whispered as her lips traced his jaw.

"I don't know..." he answered as he shut his eyes, as he let himself feel her lips on his skin. Lust pooled in his stomach, both in part to the fresh feeding and because...

Eden was most desirable.

"But I think you do. I think you know the reason. But you do not have to be afraid." She set her hands on the side of his face, looking into his eyes once more with something he'd never seen before. Understanding.

"It does not have to mean anything. It is a natural part of who we are." Her words were thickening the silence in the air between them.

Cassius ran his fingers through her hair, his gaze dipping to her crimson, blood-stained lips.

"But that is the thing, Edie. I want it to mean something. I want it to mean something to you, because it means something to me."

His words left a heavy silence between them, and for a moment Cassius thought he'd said the wrong thing. He'd opened up and told her the truth, and she...

Eden pulled him close once more and kissed him with the fire of a thousand suns.

Her tongue stroked his fangs as her fingernails traced down his arms, digging into his skin. The taste of blood on her tongue, her scent of roses and vanilla, intoxicating.

She turned him against the poster of the king size bed, his back smacking hard against it.

And where he expected to feel thrall, there was none.

Every time they'd gotten close, this close... the walls went up. The thrall stopped him. He was powerless against it, and though he knew the act of her doing so was more than illegal, he'd understood. He'd come too close, and she could not let him in.

But in this moment, there was no thrall.

Just the feel of Eden's soft, pillowy lips on his; her nails digging into his skin hard enough he knew she'd draw blood.

But he didn't care. Because her words stopped all time and space.

"How do you do that?" she whispered against his lips.

"Do what?" His voice was dark, even to his own ears.

"How do you ignite this desire within me? These things that have been long dead that I never thought I could feel again. This need, this insatiable hunger to be more?"

Cassius looked at the vampiress

before him, and he did not see a vampire.

He saw a fighter.

A woman who'd been knocked down countless times, who held secrets and was ambitious.

A force to be reckoned with.

He saw a burning fire, and the beauty of its flames entranced him.

For he burned, too.

He burned with the fire of pain, of loss, guilt, and hope that one day he would find someone who could take it all away.

And in that moment, he was certain Eden Boracelli was that person.

So he kissed her with all the fire he could conjure, letting desire and bloodlust overtake him, for though he was a creature of the night, he was still at the core of all things, a man.

A man with hopes, desires, and needs.

"Edie, my dear. You are more. You are more than anyone, especially someone like me, deserves."

"I think that is the bloodlust talking," she teased.

"Maybe it is. Maybe it isn't, but a vampire once told me to fight our instincts is insanity. To give in... to give in is salvation."

Eden's lips curved into a wicked smile as she ran her fingernails over his chest, looking up at him with dark eyes.

"If it is salvation you seek, darling, then your submission means more to me than you will ever know."

Cassius sat up in bed, raking his hand through his hair. The memories were too strong here, and he did not want to relive them.

For they were all lies.

Lies Eden had fed him for so many years. He'd thought perhaps despite all of the turmoil, the rumors, the deaths they'd both endured... even the infidelity...

He'd thought she loved him.

Because he so desperately wanted to believe it.

Because he loved her.

You loved the mask she wore.

The lies.

Everything was a lie!

Cassius threw the covers off of him, and wandered over to his suitcase, agitated. There would be no sleep tonight. Not here, not now, not in this prison of memories.

I need to get out of this house...

A knock on the door pulled him from his thoughts.

"Cassius..." the sweet voice was most recognizable, and Cassius let out a sigh of annoyance. Of course, Cora would have impeccable timing.

"Yes, Cora?" he drawled.

Cora entered the room wearing a form-fitting black dress and stilettos, her bright red hair tumbling over her shoulders in candy apple waves. With her bright blue eyes, she looked quite stunning, but her features were soft. They would always be so, thanks to the vampirism in her blood and the fact she would be frozen forever in the youth of a sixteen-year-old.

"If you want access to the den, all you have to do is ask me, you know."

Cassius turned to face her, his blood

cold.

"I beg your pardon?"

"RJ told me you were asking about the den."

"RJ?"

"The bartender from the club. Don't even try to deny it. I saw you there, talking to him."

Cassius crossed his arms, never moving from his spot.

Cora slowly padded closer, her heels click-clacking on the parquet.

"Ah. The bartender. Chatty guy, isn't he?" Cassius raised an eyebrow.

Cora was now only inches away, and he stood perfectly still.

She looked at him with a doe-eyed expression he was certain worked on many men but would not work on him in the least. Because Cassius would never see Cora the way she wanted him to, even in the light of a blood den.

"Seven-thirty," she whispered.

Cassius glanced down at her. "Come again?"

"I will grant you access to the blood den. Under one condition."

"And what is the price for this... access?"

"A date."

Cassius laughed, rolling his eyes. "Cora..."

Cora held up her hand to stop him.

"You will be ready at seven-thirty. We will go to dinner, you will pay, and then we shall attend the club, and I will grant you whatever access it is you seek to help build a case to prove Leon's got nothing to do with those murders."

Cassius blinked at her words. He'd

never known Cora to be so forward, but it had been many years since he'd seen her, spoken with her.

People really do change.

Once her words finally hit him, his eyes widened in surprise. "Murders? I thought it was only one..."

"Another girl showed up dead last night."

Cassius sighed, weighing his options. He could just ask Leon for access to the den himself, if he could get a hold of him.

Since his arrival and their initial chat on the veranda, Leon seemed to be making himself scarce. He'd always been a bit of an introvert, favoring his books and academic research more than socializing with the vampires in the covens, but even this seemed slightly out of character for him.

No, Cora was likely right. His best chance to get into the den was her. After all, next to Leon, she was the rightful heir to the properties he held. It only made sense that she would have access most others wouldn't on Leon's payroll and making a reservation with Louie was a fifty-fifty shot, especially if they did not believe Cassius's claim of friendship was sound.

Regrettably, Cassius had to agree.

"I will take you to dinner, but it is not a date," he said sternly. The wicked smile that graced Cora's lips reminded him of a devilish queen, who smiled every time she won the argument.

"Whatever you say, Cassius," Cora said as she spun around on her heels, exiting the guest room.

When she was gone, he grabbed his suitcase, and headed out of the luxurious, haunted mansion in search of a vacancy anywhere but where the ghosts of his pasts would find him.

CHAPTER NINETEEN

THE PANEL HADN'T proved as interesting as Ava would have hoped. Rather than answer questions about vampires or his research, Sam and the panel discussed the upcoming documentary and pored over legends and myths Ava already knew like the back of her hand.

But it didn't matter what he said. Not really. Ava knew it was a stretch to think he'd mention anything about the way vampires lived, let alone know anything about their marks, and though she was well versed in lore and legend, she could have listened to the man read the phone book and been invested.

There was something about his voice, its tone, volume. It was silky, hypnotizing almost. Even in a crowded room, somehow, Sam commanded the floor as if he was the only one there, but alone...

Ava could not deny she wanted more of the pleasure she'd felt with Sam, which was why, as soon as the panel had ended and everyone had gotten up from their seats, she pushed past Dallas toward the aisle.

"Excuse you," he said gruffly, but she did not care.

She only had one goal.

To make it to Sam before he left the room.

She pushed against the crowd like a salmon swimming upstream.

"Sam!" she yelled over the chatter, just as he was taking a drink from his water bottle. Security, who she hadn't noticed prior, took a step forward, but instead of completing their step, Sam halted them with his hand.

"It's okay, I got this, fellas," he said as he smirked at Ava, nodding for her to approach.

The other cast members rolled their eyes, but did not say anything, which annoyed Ava. She was not some rabid fan looking for an impromptu meet and greet. The man *did* have her belongings, after all.

"Ava, to what do I owe the pleasure?" he said as he stroked his lips with his thumb, dark eyes alighting with interest.

"I believe you have something that belongs to me," she said as she crossed her arms and raised an eyebrow at him. Just as she spoke the words, she could feel eyes on her, watching her.

Familiar eyes.

Jealous eyes.

She refused to turn around and meet the gaze of the perturbed owner. He would have to wait.

"Oh, do I now? And what might I have that belongs to you?"

"My skull clutch. It has my hotel card in it, and obviously my ID, cash..."

"Had you not left in such a hurry,

perhaps, you would not have forgotten it."

"I did not leave in a hurry..."

"I must say, I am rather used to waking up alone, but I had hoped we could have had a repeat this morning..." he said with a wink.

Ava smiled as she leaned closer, breathing in his sweet, masculine cedar scent.

God does he smell good...

"You know the definition of insanity is repeating the same thing over and over and expecting different results," she said sweetly.

Sam leaned closer to her, close enough he brought his lips to her ear, his voice dark and deep.

Like forbidden fruit.

She bit her lip to refrain from letting

out any sort of sound that would alert him to the effect he seemed to have on her. Her insides twisting with the familiar warmth all over again.

"I guarantee, Ava, that some things are best enjoyed over and over again." His voice was thick with lust.

Ava looked up at him, and the world seemed to get foggy again. It was as if a haze of lust had replaced all sense and she did not care they were in public. If Sam Kingsley did not take her right here against the stage, she felt as if she would die on the spot. Such things should have alarmed her, but they did not, for Ava was not in her right mind.

"Ahem," Dallas's voice boomed not far from her, cutting through the fog.

Ava blinked furiously, her lips straining into a thin line.

Dallas...

Realization overcame her and, suddenly, she remembered where they were, and who she was with.

What the fuck, Dallas...

Not now...

"I believe your harem is calling you," Sam teased as he kissed the underside of her ear.

"When can I see you again?" she whispered huskily, her eyes never leaving his.

Sam smiled a most sensual smile that turned the butterflies in her stomach once more.

"Meet me at my hotel room in an hour. I believe you know the way."

Ava smiled, her insides doing flips at the thought of seeing this man again, all clutches be damned.

"Yes, sir," she said sweetly as she broke away from his proximity, and headed toward a group of shocked hunters who looked like they'd just seen a ghost.

CHAPTER TWENTY

"SO, THAT'S WHAT you were doing on the other side of the hotel," Dallas snapped.

Ava sighed indignantly as she kept walking.

"You could do better, you know," Tito said nonchalantly, Hunter jabbing him in the arm.

"What? It is true…"

Ava stopped abruptly, turning to face the group of hunters, who she suddenly wished she could erase from existence at this moment.

"I didn't ask for opinions from the fucking peanut gallery, thank you very much."

"Isn't Sam a little… old for you?" Vinny said cautiously.

Ava glared at him.

At all of them, really.

"I don't need to explain my life, especially my sex life, to any of you. This conversation is over."

"Good. No offense, but we've got bigger problems than who's tapping your ass," Tito said, rolling his eyes.

"What's that?" Hunter asked curiously as Tito tapped away at his phone.

"I just got a tip from a friend, something I think might explain the vampire reports, the murders around here..."

"Well, don't just stand there like a stone, spill," Ava said, crossing her arms. A part of her was glad in that moment the conversation had shifted to something much more comfortable.

It wasn't as if Ava was ashamed of her attractions, or her choices. Something about the idea of having to explain herself to a group of men just made her feel angry and agitated. No one would bat an eye if the situation was reversed and any one of them were in her place and Sam was some model or stripper.

Besides, it didn't matter how *old* Sam

was. Age was just a number. She was over the age of eighteen, after all, and it wasn't as if she was being taken advantage of or naive or anything.

She knew exactly what she was doing.

"There's a hot spot nearby," Tito started to speak.

"A nest?" Vinny cut in again, taking his spot next to Ava, sliding his hands into the pockets of his black jeans.

"Worse." Tito shook his head.

"What's worse than a nest?" Ava asked, looking back and forth from Tito to Hunter to Vinny—ignoring Dallas altogether.

"A blood den."

Gasps erupted around Ava, and also a string of curses.

"What the hell is a blood den?" she

asked, both intrigued and annoyed. If their reaction was any indication, it obviously wasn't good, but she needed to know, especially, if it was something she needed to be on the defense about.

"Bloodsucking whorehouses," Dallas growled, and Ava realized he was beside her, flanking her opposite of Vinny, who had gone pale.

"Where there are dens, death usually follows. Vampires are known not to be able to keep their fangs or their dicks to themselves," Hunter drawled.

"It's not something we have seen a lot of, most of them were wiped out back in the early 1900s, but some are still rumored to exist across the country in pockets. Guess we found one of the remaining ones," Tito said, twisting his lips. "The sole purpose of a blood den is to provide slaves for the vamps to feast on as well as..."

"I think I get the picture," Ava said with a huff, holding up her hand.

"And you're sure there's one here?" Hunter asked.

"Well, my friend isn't usually wrong and he says there is. A place called The Dark Hearts Club. It's a couple blocks away from the hotel," Tito stated.

"Should we check it out? See if we can make a bust? Maybe find the vamp responsible for the murders? Or at the very least, I mean, we could probably put a stake through one or two and do the world a favor. Maybe if we're lucky we'll find an actual nest." Hunter's eyes crinkled in the corners as his smile spread over his face, and Ava noticed the smile on Tito's in return.

"We should definitely check it out. Do some poking around. Might find something useful, might pick off a few ticks in the process." Vinny nodded in agreement.

"Sounds good to me. When should we head over there?" Dallas said, shifting his weight.

"According to Google, the place opens at seven," Tito said.

"Um, there is no *we*," Ava said, glancing at Dallas for only a moment when she was certain he wasn't looking. This close to her, she could smell his natural scent, and it wasn't terrible. In fact, his spicy scent made her feel relaxed, and she could remember the last time she'd been this close, the last time she'd smelled him like this... She'd wanted nothing more than to fall in his arms and sleep like the dead.

And the haze that had started to form over her once again made her feel as if she could do the same again.

"Don't tell me you have plans with Doc Hollywood?" Dallas bit at her.

"Actually, I was hoping to check out this ghost tour tonight..."

"If it's ghosts you want, Kitten, I can save you the five hundred dollar ticket and show you some real haunts."

Ava pursed her lips. The premise *did* sound rather intriguing. A blood den... a place vampires could go to fulfill their hunger, their desires? Hunting vampires in their own territory? Where they'd least expect it? It would be like taking candy from a baby, and Ava had to admit her fingers twitched at the very mention of going and casing a place likely riddled with vampires.

"I mean, you don't *have* to come, but we could always use some extra back up," Vinny said with a friendly smile.

"I'll think about it," Ava said with a smile of her own as she turned and headed for the escalator.

Just when she thought she'd escaped entirely without argument, Dallas pulled her by the shoulder, turning her around forcibly on the escalator stairs.

"What is your fucking problem? You've had an attitude ever since I woke up today," Ava said angrily to Dallas.

"Me? I'm the one with the attitude? Oh, please. You've been in a bitchy mood since I fucking arrived."

"Gee, that sounds like maybe you're part of the problem, don't you think?" She turned away from him once more.

"You are infuriating, you know that!" Dallas snapped again.

"I'm infuriating?" Ava gasped in shock as she raced off the escalator as it came to the end, letting them both off on the floor.

She turned around and pointed her finger directly at him, poking him in the chest.

"You are the one who fucking kissed *me*, then left without a god damn word for two fucking years, and then you show up here and—"

"And what, Ava? It's not like I was planning on running into you or your brother when I took this gig with the guys."

"You had your chance, Dallas."

"I didn't know you were giving me a chance, Ava. So that hardly feels fair."

"My bad, I assumed grabbing you by your fucking balls was a pretty clear invitation."

A few congoers passing them by shot wide-eyed looks their way. Dallas ran a hand through his hair, his lips tightening into a straight line.

"I—"

"What? What's your excuse now, huh? Going to tell me you wanted to protect my god damn virtue or some shit? Because if that's the case, you're really late to the party on that one."

"I was trying to be respectful of your feelings and boundaries. You just lost your boyfriend..."

Dallas's words hit Ava, and the memories came flooding back.

The memory of Ross's body on the floor, bled dry, his eyes vacant.

The sound of his moan of pleasure as the vampire bit him, sucked his blood down like a bottle of beer.

She pushed them back, not wanting to fall into the hole of that darkness again. The nightmares still plagued her quite frequently.

She didn't want to remember that night.

The night she almost died.

The night Cassius saved my life.

Ava looked up into Dallas's eyes and in them she could see many things, but the most prominent was pain and regret.

Did he regret what had happened between them?

Did she?

"You don't get to do this."

"Do what, Kitten?" Dallas's voice had taken on a calmer tone as they stood head-to-head, or more accurately, as Ava stood head to Dallas's chest.

"You don't get to start this fire then douse it with water, only to spark up the embers whenever you feel like it. You can't just waltz in and out of people's lives and expect there to be no consequences."

"And you can't just hop from dick to dick in hopes you'll forget the shit you're running from. It doesn't work. Trust me, I know."

Ava scoffed and let out a small laugh. "Awww, have you and Mal finally taken your bromance to the next level? I'm so happy for you."

"Shut the fuck up, Ava."

"Make me, Dallas." She glared at him with a challenge.

"Do not push me," he growled.

"You're all bark and no bite, anyway," she said as she moved to turn around, but Dallas caught her by the wrist.

His grip around her was tight, and he pulled her back, the motion landing her right against his chest. His right hand slid around her waist, holding her flush to his body, while his left traveled up her back, sending a shiver down her spine. His fingers found the edges of her hair and he wrapped the ends around his fist, yanking on her hair and forcing her to look up at him.

Lust started to pool in Ava's stomach once more, her heartbeat pounding in her chest. And when she looked into Dallas's deep blue eyes, she couldn't deny the fire in them. For not only were Dallas's eyes full of flame and fury, but she could see her own flames staring back at her in the reflection of his irises.

Jake Dallas seemed to have a way of getting under her skin like no one else was capable of doing. So when Dallas brought his lips to his hers, instead of drowning out the fire, a new spark formed. It caught on brittle branches, on the last bits of dead leaves that lay in the memory of two years ago. And though Ava knew she should push him away, slap him, tell him to fuck off, and leave her be... She could not fight the magnetic pull of this man who both infuriated her and awakened her all at the same time.

Ava kissed Dallas back, her tongue caressing his as a soft sound of contentment escaped her lips.

His fingers tightened their grip in her hair, and it stung. His body pressed against hers was warm and solid as Ava slid her hands down his side, fingers resting on the waistband of his jeans, traipsing down his thighs.

It was the most effective way of shutting her up, and, for the moment, Ava didn't fight it. Instead, she let Dallas lead her into the darkness, into the space between what was and what could be. But the moment was too short-lived as a vibration against her thigh broke the spell over her.

"Fuck," Dallas growled as he pulled away from her. He looked back into her eyes, and the unspoken words hung between them.

This isn't over.

Far from it.

"Hello?" he said gruffly into the phone. It took all of one second for his tone, his demeanor to completely shift, and one word; one name for Ava to understand why.

"Mal? Where the fuck you been?"

***

Ava knocked on Sam's door not once, but twice. The silent pause as she waited made her feel some sting of anxiety.

What if he wasn't here?

What if he was playing some kind of cruel joke?

What if he didn't really intend on giving her stuff back?

But before Ava could fabricate another unlikely scenario, the door opened to reveal a rather delicious sight.

Sam stood in the doorway, his dark hair slightly disheveled, his warm eyes sparkling with mischief. He smirked at her devilishly, and for a moment Ava felt as if she couldn't breathe. The sight of him leaning in the doorway and his long, defined arms the only barrier between them.

"Hello, Ava," Sam said smoothly, and the sound of his voice was like melted butter. It reminded her of someone else's voice, someone she could not quite remember at the moment...

The twist in her stomach, the heat between her legs was almost instant.

How the fuck does he do that?

I'm not usually this easy around men... but it's like ever since I arrived at this damn convention...

"Hey..." she said with a smile, feeling almost giddy. She could not take her eyes off this man, and it was as if she was waiting for something, but she couldn't be sure what it was.

"Come on in," Sam said with a raise of his eyebrow, motioning her to come into the room.

Ava had the strangest feeling she was crossing some sort of line, some invisible threshold she didn't remember existed. So, she stepped into the room one foot at a time, and within seconds the door closed, sealing them both in. The curtains were closed, only a sliver of light exposed around the window's edges, which lit up the room in a velvet-red glow. The lamplights were on, on the lowest setting, also adding to the dark, somewhat hellish landscape.

Ava's gaze settled on the bureau, where her skull clutch lay perfectly untouched, perfectly kept. She walked over and grabbed it, opening it quickly to check and make sure everything was there, just as Sam came up behind her.

"It's all there, I promise," he said smoothly, his fingers tracing over the soft skin of her neck. Ava closed her eyes, breathing in the warm, cozy fireside scent of him as he surrounded her, and the reaction was instinctual. She rolled her head back against his chest, her hands settling the clutch on the bureau once more.

Sam's fingers traced down her chilled arms, his fingers brushing over her knuckles, entwining with hers, gently pushing the clutch away. His hands against hers were warm. In fact, it seemed as if heat radiated from his palms outward, heating her entire body.

"O... okay..." she said, trying to find the words. Her head was spinning once more.

"Mmmm, your lust smells delicious." Sam breathed huskily, his tongue lapping against the taut skin of her neck.

Ava's heart pounded, her legs tightened, and resistance was futile.

"Yeah? You don't smell too bad yourself." She could hear the lust in her own voice as she spoke the words.

Sam pressed his body harder against hers, sandwiching her between the bureau and his warm, solid body. He wrapped one hand around her throat, while the other trailed over the exposed cleavage of her tank top, over her breasts and down her abdomen. His fingers slowly caressed her thighs before sliding between them, pushing apart her legs with urgency. His fingers brushed over her apex, and she could feel the heat coming from his touch, the heat he seemed to be able to pull from her body.

"You are so responsive to me... I have to say, I enjoy that very much."

The words disappeared in the air as Ava settled her hand over top of his, pushing him further below, to stroke her.

"And so impatient." Sam's voice took on a hypnotic tone again, and she almost could have sworn he *hissed*.

Like a snake.

But her brain was foggy, and nothing made sense. Nothing but the insatiable need to feel Sam every way she could, until he was buried so deep within her he'd be a part of her, and even then, it wouldn't be enough.

She'd still want *more*.

He held her wrist in his hand delicately, his thumb brushing over the scar that would always be there now.

"Sam..." she groaned. The feeling as he brushed over her scar sent a shiver up her spine. "Don't be such a damn twat tease."

Sam let out a dark chuckle as he removed his hand from her throat and slid it down her back, before circling around and deftly working at the button of her jeans.

"And that mouth. Gods, I haven't had anyone tell me what to do in ages. I kind of like it."

Ava felt her internal temperature start to heat once more, and she removed her shirt instantly, a heavy sheen of sweat burgeoning on her skin. Aside from the mark on her wrist, every other bit of her felt practically combustible.

"Is it hot in here or is it just me?" she teased.

"I believe it is *us, meum delicium.*"

"What did you say?" Ava blinked as Sam slid her jeans down to the floor.

"*Meum delicium...*" he purred against her ear, his voice vibrating all throughout her body. His fingers slid between the straps of her underwear, sliding them down to the floor with ease until she was naked from the waist down, pressed against the bureau with the heat of Sam Kingsley behind her.

"What... what does that mean?" Ava breathed huskily, trying to find her breath and stability. She felt lightheaded.

The sound of a belt buckle and

shifting clothing sounded behind her loud like a church bell.

There was a moment of silence before Ava felt warm fingers pushing their way into her slick opening, felt a hardness pressing against the seam of her ass. She could not contain the moan that escaped her mouth, or the shockwave of pleasure that rippled through her as she brushed against his fingers, which stroked her with a slow rhythm, with instinct. Her fingers grasped the edge of the bureau; only to keep herself from falling.

"It means... my pleasure." Sam's tongue stroked her ear, and Ava noted it felt... different.

Different than the last time.

His voice was still hypnotic, but the *hiss* of the way he said his s's... the word pleasure... was like a snake.

Something was off.

With his free hand, he grasped her wrist once more, bringing it up to his lips. His tongue licked at the scar, and the chill returned.

But Ava could not care about such things, right now. Right now, there was only one need, one desire that filled her brain.

"I need more..." Ava said without thinking.

"You *need* more?" Sam pulled his occupied fingers back, the emptiness striking Ava like a barren desert.

"Yes, I... I need you inside me..." She struggled to speak, her brain a foggy mess, her body nothing but sensation.

Sam let out a dark sound, a sound Ava could not distinguish. His teeth nipped at the taut skin of her wrist, and the feel struck a chord deep within her.

Why did that feel so familiar?

"You are bound..." his voice wavered only slightly, and Ava felt flush with warmth at the words.

"Yes," she breathed without thinking.

"How very interesting." Sam's lips curved into a smile as he brought them against her neck, letting his tongue lave over her skin.

"Tell me, Ava... tell me what you desire most..." he purred.

Ava moaned in response, trying to find stability to answer him.

"I..." Ava found it difficult to form words.

"Tell me... let me in and I will give you *everything* you ask for, *meum delicium*."

His lips settled on her neck, his

tongue stroking her skin once more, and Ava let out a strangled moan. Something about his words seemed alarming, but she couldn't quite place what it was.

Let me in...

It was as if his voice was a thickening fog of its own, surrounding her, invading her thoughts and every beat of her heart—making it hard to breathe, hard to concentrate.

"I want to be bitten," she whispered the words like a prayer.

"Hmmm... I sense the weight of this desire... this lust for blood... it drags you down, doesn't it?"

Sam's hands left her body only for a moment, and she missed the feeling. He unclasped her bra and let it fall to the ground before his fingers softly pulled at her nipples, eliciting another moan of pleasure from her.

"You chase after anything to dull the ache, the pain... because you want it..."

"Yes..." Ava responded without thinking.

"You want it so bad, but you know it is wrong, don't you?"

"Yes."

"And what would you do if I told you I could make it all go away?"

Ava sighed as her head rolled back against Sam's chest as the world spun around her. Yet, his smooth, decadent voice kept talking, and it sounded so serene. Like someone else... someone she couldn't quite place, but whose voice could also melt the ice within her veins.

"You think about it all the time, don't you? In the darkness, it's him you want. Filling your brain, your every desire. You want the bite." Sam's voice was dark and hypnotic, and Ava was certain she would have given this man the winning lottery numbers if she had them. She was putty in his hands, a puddle of desire and lust, and yet...

Release was still so far away on the horizon.

Would she reach it?

Or would she only chase the dream of it, at the mercy of this man who fueled a hurricane of lust within her?

How is it he seemed to elicit this willingness from her?

It was almost as if she was under a spell, a spell that smelled strangely of fire and caramel and everything, every man she'd ever wanted in her life... Yet, their names were on the tip of her tongue, but she could not remember them, because there was only...

Sam.

"Yes..." she moaned. Images of glowing green eyes pushed forth in her brain, and they felt familiar, almost like she knew the owner, but like her pleasure, the name was only on the horizon, and she could not reach it. But the thought of those eyes staring into her soul from above, watching her face twist into an expression of utter ecstasy, caused her insides to twist with pleasure once more.

"Oh, Ava... you are perfect. It is as if you were made for me..." Sam whispered before pulling his hands away from her.

In the wake of their exit, she felt chilled, exposed. Every nerve was on fire, begging to be touched once again, to be brought to release. And as the emptiness overcame her, it was soon forgotten, for when Sam Kingsley pushed himself inside of her, sliding in with much ease, Ava could not think about anything but the maddening sensation of him within her.

"I want to taste you, *meum delicium*."

"Sam..." she groaned.

"Mea..." he growled darkly in response.

Ava was certain he was speaking Latin, but she was not fluent in such languages, therefore she dismissed his plea, his declaration. She could not discern what it was he was truly asking.

For she was not in her right mind, under the spell of Sam Kingsley.

Her pleasure was his, and she would have done anything to stay in that moment, to feel what he made her feel.

She could not find the words to speak, and instead, a satisfied grunt left her throat.

The bureau clicked and clacked, screeching with every thrust from Sam, and Ava gripped on for dear life as he quickened his pace. The sounds of wet skin slapping, of the creak of wood against the floor, of deep, throaty moans filled the hot room.

"*Mea voluptus unica,* Ava," he hissed in her ear, and the sound was pure heaven, dragging Ava down into Hell as her body pulsed around his, pleasure so intense she was certain she would die in its wake, and become nothing but...

Meum delicium.

My pleasure.

And when the moment had passed, Sam Kingsley slid out of her, and Ava dropped to the floor in a heap of exhaustion, sleep overcoming her once more.

***

Ava awoke in a hotel bed, naked. She sat upright, the memory hitting her like a flashback on a television show. She looked around, expecting to find Sam Kingsley, but was alone.

Alone in his hotel room.

She ran a hand through her hair, as reality set in.

She and Sam had...

Again.

Her head was pounding, as was the rest of her body. Her knees and legs felt sore as well, and she closed her eyes, taking a deep breath.

What did this mean?

Were they just... fuck buddies?

Could this... whatever crazy connection *this* was between them—could it be something more?

Sam's words echoed in her brain, *mea voluptus unica.*

Ava wasn't very keen on Latin, but something about the words made her feel somewhat suspicious.

What did they mean?

Was it some kind of blessing or curse?

Sam had uttered the words in the midst of his release, maybe it was some term of endearment like, "I love you."

Which in itself would be a good thing, right?

Celebrities *could* fall in love with fans, right?

But even as Ava thought the words,

they made her tense.

She liked Sam, she'd always liked him on television, and in person he seemed like a nice guy, but then again, they hadn't done much talking since the night at Hamlet's only two days ago.

A blush creeped onto her cheeks at the realization. Perhaps, they didn't need to talk. The connection they shared was much deeper than words, anyway, and Ava couldn't deny it spawned a hunger within her.

She had been bitten by Sam Kingsley and she did not want to give up this feeling, this excitement so soon.

She turned to swing her legs out of bed, only to see a note written on the hotel notepad, taped to the lamp.

I had a panel to attend, and I did not want to wake you. You looked too cute asleep, and I wish I could have stayed, but duty calls. This might sound forward, and I'm not really good at this stuff but... I want to see you again. Maybe we could get dinner tonight? Seven p.m.? If you agree, meet me in the lobby at six thirty.

I hope to see you, meum delicium.

— Sam

Ava's lips formed a wide, giddy grin as she stroked her fingers over the dried ink.

Maybe she was right.

Maybe this could be *more*.

The ghost hunt could wait.

There would be others.

The Dark Hearts Club could wait.

There would always be vampires, that she was most sure of, but there would never be another Sam Kingsley. There would never be another moment like this, and if life had taught Ava anything, it was to seize the moment.

So, as Ava dressed herself in Sam Kingsley's hotel room, she decided she would do just that.

CHAPTER TWENTY-ONE

CASSIUS WALKED WITH his suitcase in hand, and it reminded him of his first train ride from the sandy beaches of Portofino to Paris.

He'd only brought one suitcase then, packed with not much more than one suit and a few personal belongings. A pair of pants, a change of shirt. He had not intended on being gone much longer than a few days in Paris with Eden and Octavius, no inkling in the world all that would transpire from the moment he walked off the train.

He'd had every intention of returning to his meager apartment in Portofino, but after the coronation of Amora Medici, he'd found himself unable to leave the great city of Paris.

Not much had changed in over a hundred years for Cassius. He still stood with one suitcase, a fancy suit and a change of pants and shirts with scarce personal belongings.

But he was wiser now, older.

He'd accumulated more than wealth, he'd accumulated memories.

Memories that would not leave him be.

Still, Cassius moved with purpose, only stopping dead in his tracks when he saw a familiar face in line for the coffee cart in the small park.

"I do not recall you being a fan of coffee," he said with a friendly smile. Leon turned, startled for a moment until he set his eyes on Cassius and relaxed once he'd realize who he was.

"Cassius, how nice to see you out and about on such a lovely day," Leon said with a smirk. It was a chilly, gloomy day in Ansley, most perfect for the ambiance of a haunted town such as itself.

"Yes, well, could not sleep, I suppose."

Leon's gaze shot down to Cassius's suitcase. "Leaving so soon, are you?"

"I appreciate your letting me stay on the premises but—"

"Well, this should be good." Leon grabbed his coffee from the call out window, taking a long sip as Cassius took a deep breath.

"But I cannot stay in your home. There are far too many memories, too many ghosts within your walls."

"How long has it been since you've seen her?"

"Leon…"

"How long, Cassius?" Leon did not raise his voice, only kept it plain and solid.

"Long enough."

Thirty-seven years.

"And yet, you still can't face your demons."

"I have no demons to face, Leon. Eden is the one with blood on her hands, not I."

"Our demons are not always recognizable to us, you know. Sometimes, they come in the form of what we know best. They do not come from the world around us, but from within us."

"Yes, well they don't speak quite as loud when I am far away from all of this."

"I understand. I do wish you'd change your mind, but I digress. As long as you are comfortable and happy, Cassius."

"I would be much happier if I could get a decent meal," Cassius grumbled.

"Ah, yes. Cora told me the two of you are going out for a night of Ansley's tip-top culinary delights."

"Yes, well, she insisted."

"Nevertheless, I am sure you will find something that fits your... preferences at the den, thereafter."

"I am not partaking in the den's refreshment. I only want to observe. Perhaps, there is something that can help us find the evidence you need."

"I seem to remember you felt differently in Paris." Leon's eyes furrowed in confusion.

"I was a different man then, Leon. That was over a hundred years ago."

"And what of the man you are now?" Leon said as they strolled through the park to a bench, where Leon sat down.

"Is this... new man... content with his solace?"

"Enough. I only require that you point me to the nearest morgue, so that I may be fed and content."

"The morgue?" Leon wrinkled his nose in disgust.

"I have not had fresh blood since I left... her. In Massachusetts."

"Dear God, you don't mean to tell me you've been drinking..." Leon tilted his head to the side, curiously.

"Corpse blood, yes, Leon."

"Corpse blood?" Leon said, raising his eyebrow.

Cassius shrugged.

"That's nearly fifty years you haven't had a drop of fresh human blood." Leon's eyes lit with excitement, and Cassius wondered if disclosing such information was a good idea. He'd known Leon long enough to know the look on his face meant the gears were turning and soon he'd be subjected to a hundred questions for "research."

"Fascinating. How do you do it? Is it an acquired taste? Do you still long for the real thing or do you not remember how it tastes, memory fuddled by cold blood?"

Cassius pursed his lips, but he figured it was no use, and so he gave up standing and sat next to Leon.

"I have a man who works in the coroner's office. His name is Bryan. I saved him, but the circumstances of how I did so..."

"Exposed what you were, ah, yes. Isn't that always the case."

Cassius sighed, nodding in agreement. "Far too much in my long life, yes, it is."

"And this Bryan? He trusts you?"

"Yes. Enough. He knows I would never harm him, and I think that is enough. He leaves the discarded blood packaged and ready for me. Usually, I can get by with the minimum, make a jug or two last for weeks. It isn't the most fulfilling diet, but it has kept me alive."

Cassius looked out against the grayed, gloomy landscape as the storm clouds rolled in above them.

"Alive. That word means something different to all of us, doesn't it?" Leon glanced down at the coffee cup in his hands.

"For the humans, it is a word they cannot describe fully what it means. They do not know what it is to truly live, their lives so short in comparison to ours. They merely exist. They do not *live*." Leon spoke with grace.

"I would argue that we do the same. Empires rise and fall, and yet, we do nothing. We do not fight or intervene. We hide in the shadows, feasting on blood like animals, driven by that one instinct in which nothing else will ever compare. How can one call that living? When death becomes no more commonplace than the Sunday paper."

"We are not all Eden, Cassius."

"I know that. But what exists in Eden... it exists in all of us, does it not?"

Leon sighed, reaching his hand out fondly, setting it on Cassius's thigh as he squeezed, forcing Cassius to look into the eyes of the man he'd come to know as more than a friend.

In the absence of his father, Leon had become that man.

"Eden Boracelli is a cautionary tale of what happens when one forgets their humanity. You, dear Cassius, are an exemplary example of who we can be if we remember it. And those that fall in between are no less good or bad. They just are who they are. Is that not enough?"

"I am not qualified to answer such a question."

Leon squeezed his leg once more before letting go.

"The morgue is about two blocks in the opposite direction. Past the Silver Starling Hotel, on the other side of Ansley, bordering Cardello."

"Thank you," Cassius said with a nod.

***

It had been too long since Cassius had infiltrated a morgue in the daytime.

He'd gone to three hotels along the way to the Silver Starling, and none had vacancy due to the TerrorCon convention.

The same TerrorCon convention Ava had mentioned.

When the pulse in his veins came back with a vengeance, the hunger was so intense, Cassius thought he may expire on the streets of Ansley.

His chest ached, his muscles tight as they all twisted around his slow beating heart, his stomach and insides. His fangs longed to push into flesh, to feel warm blood, or *any blood* at that point, and suddenly, the harmless mortals surrounding him looked more than appetizing.

But it wasn't their blood he truly desired.

No.

And when he had managed to secure

a room at the Silver Starling, he'd wondered if he should stay sequestered. If she truly was nearby, as the quickening pulse in his veins indicated...

No.

You need blood.

You need to eat.

Though the wave of nausea that overcame him at the thought of feeding was nearly too much, he knew without a doubt the only way he'd fight such sickness would be to find the morgue. How he'd get in wasn't even a thought in his mind. His only goal was to find something to sate the need, something to quench his thirst and quiet the demons inside that begged for blood.

Yet, it had almost been much too easy. He'd simply smiled at the front desk attendant, turning on his charm as he had in his younger years with Eden and Octavius, or Tajiri. He'd resorted to one of his old stories, about coming to identify a body of a loved one.

Humans rarely questioned a grief-stricken, attractive man, after all.

Though Cassius once felt disdain and shame for using his charms in such a way, life with Eden had taken that from him, too. While he valued human life and the sanctity of it, years alongside the Boracelli siblings had strengthened his ability to blend in, to pull the wool over wandering, desperate eyes.

And the satisfaction of the blood, no matter if it was cold—made all the guilt and lies worth it in the end, because it quieted the pain.

It gave him the chance to live another day.

The radiating pulse in his veins was maddening, and his stomach turned, twisting in agony as he shut the door. His mouth was so dry, he thought he'd surely crumble to ash on the sterilized morgue floor. The stench of embalming liquid and bleach was so overwhelming to him, his eyes watered.

He leaned against the counter as another wave of hunger rang through him, noting the papers laid out evenly.

Papers with pictures of victims.

The murders, he realized as he took in the sight of the photographs.

All looked to have suffered the same puncture wounds that were prevalent with vampire bites, but something else stood out to him. The markings around the neck looked like *claw* marks, not strangulations as the papers implied.

But Cassius did not have time to read the reports, not when his stomach twisted, the hunger growing more insatiable by the minute.

Cassius scanned the room, until his gaze settled on the slab in the center of the room. The air was frigid and the light fell on the corpse of a man, lighting him up like a halo, only his face visible. The white sheet covering him stared at Cassius like the fabled light, and next to him, he saw it.

A container of fresh corpse blood.

The hose was no longer attached, and it sat there, still.

Crimson and thick.

Cassius's pupils dilated at the sight, his tongue flicking out to lick his dry lips.

It had been nearly a week since he'd

last fed, and he was very hungry.

He zeroed in on his target, not even registering the toxicology report that flittered to the ground in his wake.

He wasted no time, knowing the door was locked.

He'd be quick.

His hands wrapped around the glass container, bringing it to his lips as if it was nothing more than a cherry slushie.

Cherry...

His mind hung on the word, and all the connotations that came with it.

Ava loved cherries.

Cherry pastries, cherry slushies, cherry pie with enough whip cream to be considered its own level on the food pyramid.

The thought of her pervaded his brain as he let the cold blood run down his throat, a deep groan of satisfaction escaping his lips. His head started to feel fuzzy, and he turned around, glass in hand as he leaned against the countertop, causing a cup of pens to fall over from his motion.

It wasn't the best tasting corpse blood he'd had, but it was enough. Enough to make his body heat with warmth, his cock twitch with life once more from the taste, the thoughts that bloodlust always brought him.

He closed his eyes, gulping down the thick liquid as if it were nothing more than a milkshake, careful to not let it run over his lips, down his neck; careful to avoid any evidence or staining of his clothes.

The image of her the first time he'd laid eyes on her pushed forth. The crimson streaks running down her creamy, pale thighs from the wounds in her legs. The fight in her eyes as she struggled against her own imminent death to stand, to reach out.

He'd never seen anything quite as beautiful as the sheer will, the defiant ambition that was Ava Crowley. He'd felt drawn to her in that moment, in so many unexplainable ways, like a moth to a flame.

Like Icarus, drawn to the sun.

He'd done the right thing, hadn't he?

He'd saved her life, but in return he ached with pain and desire, the intensity of the claiming bond ever present in his brain, his being.

Even now as he let the chilled, semi-congealed blood slide down his throat, he could feel her pulse within him like a beacon, and the thought of seeing her somehow, someway, was difficult to fight.

The sound of her gasp as his fangs pierced her skin only for a moment.

How her bountiful cleavage heaved with heavy breath after she'd staked Brody only two years ago.

The light catching in her eyes as she looked at him in those moments.

Black vampire blood splattered across her beautiful face and skin.

Cassius's cock hardened at the thought, the memory, and it was no use fighting. There was only one way to truly quiet the unrelenting desire that blood and thoughts of Ava brought him. Though, a strange sense of heightened urgency seemed to hit him, like the first hit of caffeine from a cup of coffee. Only this feeling was much, much more intense, and it only fueled his arousal.

His *need*.

Cassius shakily slid his hand down his leather pants, the haze around him thickening. He gripped himself tightly and let the thoughts drag him under once more, the desire in him building like a crescendo. A part of him knew every bit of what he was doing was wrong; the sane part of him.

The human part of him.

But it was as if some unknown force compelled him, some spell and control was out of his reach. The vampiric part of him did not care about right and wrong. It only cared about blood and lust. Drinking corpse blood would not erase the lust that came with drinking blood.

No.

Though, the thought of *fresh* warm blood—Ava's blood to be exact—even as he consumed his sustenance, was enough to stir the instinct, let alone the fact they were *bonded*. He'd claimed her blood as his own when he'd saved her life and knowing her blood was *his* to take... was enough to drive him mad.

He needed *release*.

He needed a quiet, serene peace. So he let go of the glass, letting it clatter against the countertop, and the euphoria of bloodlust settled over him like a velveteen blanket.

But something was off.

He'd never felt quite *this* aroused by the thoughts alone, or the corpse blood.

He opened his eyes, and the room seemed to blur, a jarring discovery.

Instinctually, he closed them once more, trying to fight the effect, and when he did so, he only saw *her*.

Ava sat on her knees before him, looking up at him through her long dark lashes. Pale and naked on the concrete floor she sat like a statue, the only light visible was the fire in her amber eyes that called to him. She looked delicate, like the goddess Venus perched on the dais, waiting for him. But he knew she was anything but delicate. She reached out for him, crooking her finger as she cast him a most wicked glare and he came to her beckon call.

In life, it seemed as if the existence of him was nothing but an annoyance to Ava. Come. Leave. Come. Leave. He was at the mercy of her command, and always would be. As long as she wore his mark, as long as her blood was *his...* He'd be a slave to Ava Crowley and all that she was. All she had to do was say the word.

"Yes," she purred in his ear as her lips hovered over his neck, as her hand traveled between them, wrapping her fingers around his thickness, squeezing tightly.

"Yes, Cassius. You can come for me, now."

CHAPTER TWENTY-TWO

CASSIUS TURNED THE corner, the overly bright fluorescent lights of the Silver Starling casting a glare directly in his eyes. His thoughts seemed to be going a mile a minute, ever since he'd broken into the morgue. He'd managed to leave without drawing too much attention, but somewhere between his exit and the few blocks it took to reach the Silver Starling, Cassius realized two things.

The first was that he'd been careless. He'd been so used to receiving purified, clean blood from Bryan that he hadn't even thought twice about checking the reports of the corpse on the slab.

Though his vampiric genes prevented him from falling ill with blood borne disease, they did not prevent him from feeling the effects of certain toxins within the blood, which led him to the second realization—the blood he'd feasted on had been laced with some kind of euphoric toxin.

Though Cassius was no stranger to alcohol or drug infused blood, something about this felt... different. He'd lived through the eighties and nineties with

Tajiri, when such drugs were frequently the cause of many deaths, cocaine and ecstasy being quite popular at the time, and he thought that must be it.

For what else *could* it be if not a drug?

He blinked furiously, as his eyesight settled, the light dissipating, shifting into sharper vision as a body came through from the ice room, nearly smacking into him. As his vision adjusted, he felt his skin crawl, his blood boiling beneath the surface as a pulse *throbbed* in his veins, louder than anything he'd ever felt before, and his eyes took in the sight before him.

Perhaps, I am hallucinating...

It was Ava, with a bucket of ice in her hands. Her short, chocolate hair was wet, and the scent of bergamot and jasmine filled his senses like the room had been sprayed, bathed in her scent. She wore nothing but a Van Halen t-shirt, large and boxy and long enough to barely be considered decent as it stopped just a hair above her mid-thighs.

He fixated on the sight, noting the flesh of her long, beautiful legs was still a tinge pink, as if she'd left the shower only moments ago. Cassius rubbed his eyes.

"What the fuck are you doing here?" Her voice was sour, like a tart cherry, but sweet to his ears.

I'm not hallucinating...

The realization hit him and he blinked, tiny spots splintering in his vision as his heart beat louder, as her pulse rocked his body. She smelled quite intoxicating, and Cassius noted another scent, not as prevalent but still quite intoxicating.

His eyes roved over Ava, settling on the hem of her t-shirt as understanding dawned on him. The scent of...

Dear lord, have I died and gone to Hell?

Think unsexy thoughts...

He felt the familiar stiffening in his groin. He groaned in defeat.

He'd already sated his hunger, his desire, hadn't he?

Cassius knew the answer, but it did not matter. For whatever toxin was laden in the corpse's blood, it seemed was only getting started and he needed to regain control.

"What's the matter? Cat got your tongue?" Ava said as she shifted her weight, raising an eyebrow at him, tapping her foot.

This is really happening...

She is here...

I am...

Cassius let out a deep sigh as he ran his hand through his hair, feeling the beginnings of sweat forming on his brow.

Out of all the hotels in Oklahoma...

"Paying a visit to an old friend." Despite feeling as if he was out of his wits, his voice did not betray him. Cassius shifted his stance behind the vending machine, the feeling of rigidity building against his leather pants again, the thrum of her pulse and the bloodlust making his throat dry with thirst, as if he hadn't fed nearly an hour ago. As if, somehow, his afternoon lunch had already metabolized through his system, leaving him vacant and ready to be filled once more.

She smirked as she held the bucket of ice in front her.

"I thought I told you to stay away," she said the words, but for once they carried no bite.

"I do have other friends, you know," he said with a smirk.

"Mhmm..." She squinted her eyes narrowly at him as if she was weighing the sincerity of his words.

"I was born at night, you know, but not last night." She twisted her lips, the motion lighting up her eyes in the fluorescent halo from above.

His vision sharpened as he found himself falling into the depths of them, fixating on the gold flecks that reminded him of a morning sunrise.

I must be dreaming if she is being this friendly.

She's never this... relaxed...

A startling thought popped into his chaotic brain as her smile elicited one from his own mouth.

Is she flirting with me?

Somewhere in his brain, he hoped she was. The thought alone that she would even entertain such a thing, *flirting* with him, would indicate that she...

Cassius could not complete the thought for all attention went to his cock, straining against his leather pants. He shifted his weight once more, propping his left leg out nonchalantly, hoping to heaven she didn't notice. If she did... Well, he would rather not die against a vending machine in Ansley,

Oklahoma.

"I didn't follow you here, Ava." Cassius shifted uncomfortably in her gaze. He felt an overwhelming desire to make her understand this. To make sure she understood he was not some stalker, not some person who disregarded her wishes at the behest of his own.

"No, it's just all some big, serendipitous miracle that we'd wind up miles away in the same fucking city." She twisted her lips, the ghost of a smirk on the edge of the corners.

"Choose to believe me or not, but this is not a pleasure call," he responded defensively. He didn't mean for his voice to sound so harsh, but the aching in his cock was beginning to border on unmanageable.

His body temperature rose, and he

swallowed nervously. A part of him longed to touch her, to know he wasn't imagining this. But the desire to brush his thumb over her bite mark, *his* bite mark, was not the only one fighting for dominance in his brain.

He longed to run his hands along the expanse of her exposed long, smooth legs and feel her pulse beneath his fingertips. He longed to run those same fingers through her soft hair, to hold her close against him and feel her life, her lips against his own... but another, the sane part of him; whatever shred was left at the moment, knew he should keep his distance.

For both of them.

Not only because he feared he may get carried away with his whims, but because he had managed to restrain himself thus far, and he did not want to falter now. The thin line he walked with Ava Crowley was a tightrope, at best, and he knew if he wanted to see her again, share coffee in the Impala, or find himself crawling in through her window at night without being staked, he would have to keep his feelings, his desires, in check. He would do whatever it took to keep his presence in her life, one that did not end up in death.

For a life without his sweet Avarice was no life at all.

Perhaps, it was the toxins making their way through his system, or wishful thinking, or perhaps, it was just a matter of serendipity, like a comet traipsing across the sky—but something about Ava felt... different.

Something had infiltrated the walls of

her fortress, and in its wake was this alluring creature who was *flirting* with him. As if she herself had been affected by some sort of spell or toxin. One that disintegrated her walls, her own misgivings and preconceived notions.

Realization dawned on him, as he hung on that word.

Toxins.

The photographs, the murders.

The bite marks, claw marks...

Leon's hunch.

Of course, it all made sense.

There was only one creature who could secrete euphoric toxins that would rival any drug, even ecstasy, and leave marks like that.

Incubi and Succubi.

Though they were hard to come by normally, unless it was mating season, which only happened every hundred years or so. Cassius closed his eyes as reality set in, as Leon's words reverberated in his brain.

There hasn't been a sighting in this area for nearly a hundred years.

His thoughts raced at the horror of what that truly meant. Leon had suggested an Incubus was responsible for the murders, yet, he had no substantial proof, needing toxicology reports.

Toxicology reports that Cassius took for granted during his luncheon.

Where there was an Incubus, there was likely a den of Succubi not far away, and if he was truly working through the effects of Succubi toxin, he knew he was in for a long ride. Such toxins usually had catastrophic effects on the mortals, who could not handle the physicality of such a creature, especially when they transitioned to their full form, and those who could handle the sexual congress become prime targets for mates to host the Succubi's essence until they overtook their male targets in every way until they became them.

Like a parasite with only one purpose—to spawn more Succubi.

Though relations between the demonic creatures and vampires wasn't likely, it was possible, and their toxins would still work their lust-fueled magic. He'd seen it before. The only difference was it would wear off quicker on him than it would on a mortal, and he would just have to ride it out until it was completely out of his system.

Before Ava could respond, the sound

of her stomach growling pulled him from his thoughts. He could have said anything, but all he settled on was, "You are hungry?"

Ava let out a soft sound of contentment.

A *laugh.*

A genuine, sweet *laugh.*

The sound was music to his ears.

"The question is not am I hungry, Cas. The question is, can I eat? And the answer to that is always *yes.*" She smiled.

She is flirting with me.

I don't believe it.

Of all the luck, the one time she lets her guard down and I'm high as a bloody kite.

Perhaps, it was the moment, the toxins. Perhaps, it was because they were in the middle of nowhere, surrounded by temptation on all sides. Cassius couldn't be sure what it was that spurred him to seize the moment.

But seize it he did.

"Donuts." His voice was starting to waver.

"What?"

"There's a place not far from here that makes the most delectable donuts. Let me take you." The words were out of his mouth before he could really hold on to them.

Her facial expression shifted to one of distrust, and her stance tensed as she grabbed the bucket tightly like a shield.

Anxiety spread through him as his heartbeat quickened, and he felt quite on the spot waiting for her answer.

Perhaps, the toxins had gone to his

brain.

Perhaps, he'd overstepped.

Before he could open his mouth to speak, to apologize, Ava spoke.

"Fine. But you try anything, and I mean *anything*—" She pointed at him with one finger. "I will fucking dust you." Her voice was solid, and the threat was real as she glared at him with warning.

Doesn't she know I would never hurt her?

The realization of her words hit him, and immediately the panic set in.

She'd said *yes.*

And that changed everything.

"You okay, Cas? You look a little... jumpy." She regarded him with a suspicious gaze.

"Scout's honor, my sweet Avarice." He smiled nervously, feeling as if his slow beating heart would jump clear out of his chest at her words.

She said yes.

"I'm going to drop this off and grab some pants. I'll meet you out here in, like, ten minutes." She was definitive in her commands.

"And your weapons," he muttered quietly. Cassius knew she did not usually leave her house, or anywhere, without at least one or two weapons of choice. Most favorably, it was two stakes and a backup pocketknife.

Ava's eyes perked up.

"Who says I'm not packing right now?" She taunted him.

"Where on earth would you be hiding a stake right now?" he said as he cocked his head curiously, his gaze once again wandering over her freshly showered form, traveling down her long, slim legs to her boots.

Ava batted her eyelashes at him as a chuckle escaped her lips.

"Wouldn't you like to know?"

Cassius watched her turn the corner, and when he was certain she was gone, only then did he remember to breathe. The dizziness overtook him as he closed his eyes, leaning against the cold ice machine.

"What the hell have I gotten myself into?"

CHAPTER TWENTY-THREE

AVA DROPPED OFF the bucket of ice abruptly, like it was a hot potato and burned her fingers.

What the hell is wrong with me?

I should be pissed.

I should stake him right here...

I should...

Ava's thoughts spiraled in all

directions, fraying at the edges. She could not pretend that Cassius's appearance meant nothing to her. She'd told him not to follow her, and whether he was telling her the truth or not about "visiting an old friend," it didn't change the fact that he was *here*. In Ansley, Oklahoma, in her hotel, offering her sugar confections.

Which he always does.

Only, this somehow felt different than all the other times he'd shown up to her Impala parked outside vacant lots at two in the morning with a bag of cookies and coffee. Something about the way his eyes looked, slightly glassy, and the way her scar *tingled* in his presence... Even the way he spoke—though his smooth, velveteen voice was still dreamy, it carried the hint of something she'd never heard in it before.

Fear.

But what on God's green earth did Cassius have to fear?

Ava removed Sam's Van Halen shirt, discarding it on the bed haphazardly; wondering for a moment if she should confiscate the thing as a souvenir. With all the other clothes strewn about his hotel room, she thought he'd likely not even notice it had gone missing but settled against the theft.

She jumped into her jeans, fastening the belt with haste as her stomach growled again.

"Shut the fuck up, you'll get yours soon enough," she grumbled in retort.

She dressed in her black tank top once again, smoothing the fabric over her abdomen. Looking herself over in the mirror, she ran her fingers through her hair, smoothing the stray locks into place before sliding her feet into her boots. Once again, she scoured the floor for her stake, and upon finding it, slid it into the side of her boot.

Whether or not Cassius was telling the truth, she could not deny the inkling in her gut that perhaps, it had *something* to do with the murders. Ava did not believe in coincidences.

The murders, the blood den, the congregation of all those vampires in one place...

I wonder what Cas knows about the blood den...

Is that why he's here?

The thought of Cassius in such a place caused a flurry of emotion in her. Anger pushed to the forefront, right behind it was envy. Her body flushed with heat, and her insides twisted at the thought. The desire to set something or *someone* aflame at the thought of Cassius's fangs in *anyone*... Ava did not want to think about it. So she pushed it away.

I'm just hangry, that's all.

Nothing more.

She grabbed the note from the lamp, shoving it in her clutch before finally leaving the aftermath of Sam Kingsley's love nest.

When she arrived back at the spot she'd left him, she was only somewhat surprised to see he was still there. A part of her thought perhaps, she'd imagined the whole thing, that perhaps, she was still asleep in Sam Kingsley's warm bed, but there was another part of her that would have *jumped* at the chance that maybe, just maybe...

Maybe he *did* follow her all the way to Ansley, Oklahoma because...

"How close is this place?" she asked before she could let her thoughts run away from her again. When Cassius was around, she found it rather easy to let them wander.

"A couple blocks," he said, sliding his hands in his pockets as he turned his back to her.

It wasn't the first time he'd done so, but something in the way he did in that moment gave Ava a startling thought.

He trusts me.

He trusts that I will not stab him in the back and turn him to dust.

But why?

Ava shook her head, dispelling the

thoughts. She was out of sorts, it seemed, ever since she'd awakened in Dallas's bed this morning. Perhaps, it was the aftereffects of her attack from that redheaded vamp. Perhaps, she *was* suffering a concussion. It would explain her sudden shift in behavior, her mood swings, and her thoughts...

"Okay. But fair warning, if I don't make it, I'm not against eating you to survive, you know," she said with a smirk. She watched Cassius's shoulders tense at her words. As he looked over his shoulder at her, his glowing green eyes sparkled with something she couldn't quite place.

"Fine by me, as long as your hunger has been abated."

Ava felt a strange pooling in her gut, a strange flush of heat radiating from her scar at his words, his gaze, and therefore, she forced herself to look away.

I think I have completely lost my fucking marbles.

They walked past the lobby, past all the signs and congoers, and Cassius seemed to be picking up pace, almost running at this point.

"Where's the fucking fire? Can you slow down?" she grumbled as she tried to keep up.

Cassius abruptly stopped, and she almost collided with him, just before the revolving doors.

"I'm sorry, I thought you could keep up," he said, flashing her a charming smile.

Ava crossed her arms.

"I can. I just didn't plan on running a

5k to the donut shop."

"Very well. I shall adapt to your leisurely pace, if it pleases you."

Ava raised her eyebrow, fighting the smile that wanted to spread over her lips. She'd never seen Cassius this at ease. Usually, he was more reserved, a bit stand-offish, even. But here, now...

He was different, and though that should have alarmed her, should have been some sort of red flag, it wasn't. In fact, she found that she enjoyed this side of Cassius, and a part of her wanted to see more of it.

No.

That's a terrible idea.

That is how he'll get you.

Pull you in and end your fucking life.

Don't fall for his charms.

He's a monster and always will be.

But yet, after two years, he hadn't made a move to bite, attack, or… anything. He'd only stood off to the side, showing up with snacks and coffee, or in the middle of the night when she'd had a nightmare.

Ava was not certain what it all meant, and so she decided to focus on the task at hand instead of the labyrinth of thoughts this strange being seemed to build in her mind.

"I… thanks. I guess," she grunted as she pushed through the revolving doors, finding their way out on the street.

It was raining, and Ava let out a curse as she realized.

"Damn it, I should have brought a hoodie."

"No need for that," Cassius said smoothly, popping an umbrella over her head.

"Where the hell did you get that, Mary Poppins?" she asked as she looked up at the golden-haired vampire who held a black umbrella over her head, shielding her from the rain. Yet, it fell on him, and the sight of water droplets running down his smooth, pale skin stirred the heat inside her once more and she had to remind herself to breathe.

Even now, wet and pale, he looked like some angel fallen from the heavens, too beautiful for a place like Ansley, sticking out like a sore thumb, like a man from another time.

Because he is a man from another time, Ava.

He's an immortal, bloodsucking monster.

"Hotels such as the Starling usually

keep a canister of available umbrellas just for this occasion."

"Oh. Guess I haven't stayed in a lot of hotels this nice."

"Neither have I."

Ava wrapped her hand around the base of the umbrella, just below his hand. She pushed only slightly toward him.

"There's enough room for the both of us," she said solidly.

Cassius's lips turned up in a smirk.

"Is that an invitation?" His gorgeous green eyes searched hers, looking for something she couldn't quite grasp.

"It's common courtesy," she retorted as he stepped closer, underneath the umbrella, a sliver of space between them.

"Such excellent manners." The sly

smile that spread on his lips exposed just a hint of his fangs, and Ava had to admit the sight was most appealing.

"Uh huh. You start running again and I might have to stake you," was all Ava could manage as they took off for the donut shop, and true to his word, he kept with her pace.

"Your wish is my command," he murmured as she dropped her hand, leading them through the rain into salvation.

"Are you enjoying your... convention?" he said the words as if he was unsure of himself, unsure whether or not she would bite him or snap at him.

A maddening flush crept up on her cheeks at his words, as images of Sam filled her brain, as her muscles strained with ache with every step, a reminder of just how much she'd enjoyed *him* and how he made her feel.

"I, uhm... guess you could say it's going pretty well. Except for the murders." She looked at Cassius, who was looking straight ahead and likely would not notice, watching his facial expression at the words.

His lips formed a thin line, but other than that, he was expressionless, unreadable.

"I must confess that is why I am here. A very good friend of mine was accused of those murders."

"Does this very good friend happen to be a vampire?"

"Yes," he answered plainly as they stopped on the corner of the street, waiting for the walk sign to light up.

"And what can you do about any of

it?" She realized the words sounded much harsher than she'd intended, but Cassius did not flinch.

"You have your skills, Ava, I have mine." The way in which he answered her forged a new path of questions, and Ava wondered momentarily what sort of *skills* someone like Cassius would have.

She followed the alluring vampire across the street, and when they came to the building, Ava felt a wave of disappointment. It was a small building, barely distinguishable as a restaurant at all, except for the window set in the dark brick that showed a lit-up dining room with hardly any individuals in it, and a neon sign that read *open.*

"This is it?" Ava asked, raising an eyebrow as Cassius closed the umbrella beside her.

"Indeed, it is." He smiled at her.

"It doesn't look like much." She shrugged as she headed for the door, but Cassius cut her off, opening it for her instead.

She rolled her eyes.

Who does he think he is, Prince Charming?

"In my experience, the best things in life are always the things we take for granted."

"Whatever, I'm starving," she said.

"That makes two of us," he said as he followed her into the light of the dining room.

CHAPTER TWENTY-FOUR

AVA SIPPED HER coffee, and Cassius leaned back in the booth languidly, thankful for the table obstructing her view.

The crash of the Succubi toxin was at its peak and would likely taper off soon. Though, at the moment, it surged through him like a buzzing vibration, alighting his nerves, making every sensation magnified—including the uncomfortable tightness in his leather pants—and the dry, scratchy feel of his throat.

Ava relaxed as she pursed her lips, reading the menu of outlandishly named confections, none the wiser.

"So, how do you know about this place?" she asked as she turned the page.

She seemed quite conversational this afternoon. Most of the time she just rolled her eyes and shirked past him as if he were nothing more than a nuisance.

"I spent some time traveling when I first came to this country from Italy," he answered. It wasn't a lie. Though, he'd left out the part about *why* he'd traveled so much after setting foot on American soil for good in the 1940s.

When he'd found Eden up against the brick by a dastardly warlock in 1923, he'd only meant to find her and bring her back to Rome, but the lure of all America had to offer, and the woman who had managed to snake her way into his bed and arms were, too difficult to leave behind.

And after the Boracellis and the High Covens had arranged their engagement, the hunt for where to lay roots was quite strenuous and long because Eden was never satisfied with any of it. The towns. Him. Nothing was good enough for Eden, and never would be... The hole in her heart could never be filled. The darkness would only consume her until nothing was left but vengeance and greed.

Cassius pushed the memories—the

thoughts of the wicked queen—out of his mind, glancing around the restaurant at the decor. It still looked just as it had in the fifties when he'd last visited it. The checkered floor was still just as shiny, the silver-edged bar bright against the faded yellow acrylic. Even the lamplights looked original, still casting their dewy glow over the pale-yellow booths and empty tables.

There were only a few people at this hour, being a few blocks from the convention and looking as quaint and unassuming as it did. Only the locals truly knew what delicacies lay behind its doors.

Eden never cared for sweets, not like he did. To her, they were merely human fodder, something that gave no value to their kind, and provided no real sustenance, and Cassius could not forgo such indulgences. Not when vampirism made everything taste better, even the most mundane of foods.

Ava settled her gaze just as the waitress came over.

"What'll it be, y'all?" she asked as she popped her bubblegum. Cassius looked at Ava, awaiting her answer.

"I'm going for a dozen. I'd like two strawberry-frosted, two chocolate, two raspberry jelly-filled, two cookies and cream and..." She looked at Cassius with a devilish smirk.

"What would you like?" she asked sweetly, but Cassius knew it was an act. Sweet and Ava Crowley were not two things that normally went together. Her tone may have been sweet, but she did not hide her sarcasm well.

He smiled just enough that the edge of his canine fangs showed only to her, and almost instantly felt the faint increase in her pulse through his veins. The notion made him feel like king of the world, knowing that even if she would not admit such things, that he did have *some* effect on her. An effect that had nothing to do with thrall.

"I'll have two of the Red Velvet Supreme," he said as calmly as he could muster.

Ava squinted at him, weighing his response once more. She said nothing as she handed the menu to the waitress. She waited until the woman left, before speaking.

"You're not going to actually eat that, are you?" She crossed her legs underneath the table, a motion which bristled her boot against his long legs, and he found himself shifting again as his desire throbbed with need at her touch.

This is madness.

You are better than this...

"Although it does not sustain me, I can eat it. I can still taste sugar, among other things," he answered.

"What were you doing before I ran into you?" The words fell out without warning.

"None of your business," she bit. Cassius watched the heat crawl into her cheeks, watched her eyes rise with surprise as if he could see into her very soul, and the walls were up once more. He could feel Ava closing up like a clam and instantly regretted his words.

"What were *you* doing before I ran

into you?" she retorted.

"Investigating." He shifted his arm so it strayed across his lap.

"Investigating? Since when do you do the Nancy Drew thing?"

"I have done the *Nancy Drew* thing for quite some time, though it has been a while. I enjoy solving puzzles, actually. Keeps my mind stimulated."

Ava scoffed and rolled her eyes. "I take it your *investigation* has to do with your 'friend'?"

Cassius nodded. As long as the conversation kept on this topic, fighting the effects of the toxin would be much easier. Procedural conversation was a mood killer, after all, no matter what century he was in.

"Yes. In fact, there is something I need to tell you about my...

investigation."

Ava raised an eyebrow, and he could tell she was weighing whether or not to take the bait. She leaned back in her booth, bouncing her leg nervously against his, and his cock twitched again.

Devil take me now.

"And what do you *need* to tell me, Cas?"

He fought the smile as she looked at him with curiosity. If there was one thing Cassius had learned about Ava in the last two years, it was that the woman had a hunger and ambition for knowledge. She soaked up the books she read like a sponge, retained even the most off-kilter facts in her head like they were required reading.

She hated to be the last to know anything, especially when it came to the supernatural. She was a Crowley, after all. Such lust for things was in her blood.

"The murders are being made to look like a vampire killing, but in fact they are not."

"And how do you know that?" she said as she took a sip of her coffee. Her tongue darted out, licking her lips of the remnants of whip cream, and Cassius had to concentrate on his words. It should not have been as difficult as it was.

"Because it is mating season for the Succubi and Incubi."

"Come again?" Ava said, nearly spitting out her coffee.

"Every hundred years, the Succubi awaken, and they seek out human males to mate with. When they find humans who are capable, they..." Cassius could feel his throat going dry, not from thirst, from slight panic.

Even his unruly member tensed, waiting for the description, the rest of the explanation, which left him feeling slightly uncomfortable.

Ava blinked, waiting for him to continue. "They what? Come on, Cas, don't stop there," she taunted him, a smirk playing on her lips.

Cassius shifted his stance, crossing his legs, and sitting up straighter, away from her incessant bouncing leg.

"When the Succubi find humans who are capable of... copulating... they... absorb the male's essence, which gives them the ability to attach themselves to the male like a... like a parasite. Eventually, they take over completely, fusing themselves with the male to become an Incubus, and when that happens, the Incubus seeks out a female mate to breed with, to spawn more Succubi for the next season, and the cycle repeats endlessly."

The air was silent between them as Ava wrinkled her nose in disgust.

"Ugh. Demon spawn. Great."

"The mating season occurs every hundred years, and Leon..." Cassius stopped as he realized he was saying too much.

"Leon's your friend, I take it."

"Yes."

"So you think the murders are what? Angry Succubi and Incubi who got carried away or something?" she asked.

"Or something. I think... I think for whatever reason, they are targeting the vampires. Though, I'm not sure why. Our kind tend to... stay away from demons."

Ava looked surprised at this revelation, and then she dropped a question Cassius did not see coming.

"What do you know about the blood den? The Dark Hearts Club?"

Cassius could feel his blood run cold.

How did Ava know about the blood den...?

"I beg your pardon..." His voice lost all its vibrancy and went flat.

"The Dark Hearts Club. Rumor has it, it is one of the only remaining dens in the country."

"It is," he answered cautiously.

"So you do know about it." She grinned.

"Leon owns it," he blurted out.

Ava nodded, just as the waitress came and dropped off a platter of confectionary delights. Her eyes looked like they were going to pop out of her head.

Cassius felt a warm smile spread across his lips at the sight, grateful for a slight reprieve from the dangerous conversation.

"Do you think the two are connected, somehow?" she asked as she took a jelly filled donut off the top of the platter.

"What do you mean?" He reached for one of the red velvet ones, his fingers brushing hers as he did so, and the touch sent a jolt of electricity directly to his groin.

"I mean, the Succubi are like, sex demons, right? And vampires go to a den for more than just blood," she said as she bit into her donut.

Cassius watched her bite into it, the red jelly clinging to her lips, and the image of her covered in blood—*vampire blood*—resurfaced. She was right, but he did not want to travel down that road of thinking. Not when the sight of red jelly all over her lips forced the memories on him with unrelenting fervor.

Her heaving chest, blood-soaked skin, eyes wild with the rush of her kill.

His cock twitched and he pursed his lips.

"Some do, yes."

Ava moaned in delight as her tongue darted out and licked the remains of jelly from her lips. Cassius stifled the reciprocal groan in his throat as he focused on his own uneaten donut, stilling his breath.

The thirst was lessening. The thirst for *blood*, that was. The thirst for Ava Crowley was only getting worse.

Maybe this was a bad idea...

"Well, I mean, it makes sense *maybe* the demon fuckers might want to use the den as hunting grounds to find their mates, and vampires can be territorial as hell."

Cassius scoffed in response. "Not all vampires are *territorial.*"

"Yes, they are." She waved him off as if his pleas were nothing, taking another bite of her donut, stuffing it in her mouth like a chipmunk. Red jelly spread on her lips once more.

"I suppose you could be on to something. I hadn't considered that the Succubi or the Incubus could be using the den to seek out their mates."

"Do they have any tells? Like, demons have red eyes, vamps have thrall..." Ava stopped, as if she was remembering where she was and who she was talking to. She took a long drink of her coffee before setting it down.

Cassius sighed.

"Well, those who do not... take the toxin *well*, the lust drives them mad, and usually a Succubi will feast on their blood."

"So they have fangs like vampires?"

"Yes. Succubi in their true form have fangs and a forked tongue and red eyes. Like traditional demons."

"What do you mean, in their true form?" Ava asked cautiously.

"They can only turn to their true form during mating. Otherwise, they look just like you or me."

"So, there's no way to tell in a crowded room who's human and who is a demon fucker?"

Cassius rolled his eyes at her coarse description. He nearly let out a laugh and would have if the conversation was not so serious. Thankfully, the toxins were thinning out and he was starting to feel slightly normal. His thirst for blood had quieted, yet, there was still the matter of his lust he'd need to take care of sooner or later.

"If there is, I'm not sure I know the answer. I haven't cavorted very much with the likes of demons. I try to stay away from such things."

"Are you going to eat that or what? You've been staring at that damn donut for at least five minutes."

"Don't even think about it. You've got

at least seven other choices on that platter to choose from." He nodded at the spectacular array of donuts in between them.

Ava narrowed her eyes at him, challenging him.

"Besides, you aren't fast enough." He smirked at her.

"Is that a challenge, Cas?" She smirked back, biting her lip. The sight was downright sinful.

They stared at each other like it was a standoff, one waiting for the other to flinch, and then make their move. And suddenly, it was as if the weight of the world had lifted and they were not in the middle of Jim Bob's Diner, as if they were not on opposite ends of the mortal slash immortal chain. It was almost as if they were just, Cassius Aurelia and Ava

Crowley, nothing more.

Their hands collided, a mass of fingers and icing, as Cassius snatched up the dessert, pulling it out of her reach. He bit into the donut, fangs and teeth piercing the soft cake, sating the desire to bite, if only for the moment. The icing on his tongue was so sweet, the taste of vanilla and cream dialed up to eleven. He swallowed the bite, casting Ava a sly smile, wearing his victory proudly.

"Your enthusiasm is endearing, my sweet Avarice." He licked his lips.

Ava's eyes sparkled with mischief.

"Who says I lost? The icing's the best part, anyway." She retorted.

Cassius shook his head as he swallowed down the sweet pastry. Ava glanced down at her icing covered fingers, before placing one directly in her mouth, and Cassius bit down harder on his donut.

He was certain if he'd had a mortal heart, it would have stopped beating on the spot at the sight of Ava's fingers in her mouth. He fixated on the way she slid them in and out over her jelly-stained lips, how her tongue wrapped around her long fingers, and Cassius could hold off no more.

"Ahem... if you'll excuse me..." He nodded over to the restrooms. He needed some distance, and it seemed like the best excuse. If he didn't leave her right now, he would be far too tempted to taste her raspberry flavored lips for himself until he'd cleaned every last drop from her luscious, divine mouth.

Ava licked the icing off her thumb,

her gaze fixed on him through long, dark, thick eyelashes.

She nodded in silent response, as Cassius all but sprinted to the restrooms.

CHAPTER TWENTY-FIVE

AVA PICKED APART a frosted donut, savoring the sweet taste; hungry for more. It was almost as if she was starving for something she couldn't quite put her finger on.

Well, I guess I haven't really eaten much in the last couple days...

The realization struck her like a

bucket of ice water. Normally, when she'd travel to a new place, the first thing she did was scope out the local cuisine, but she hadn't thought much of food, or anything really, since she'd met Sam Kingsley at Hamlet's merely forty-eight hours ago.

Well, the man is quite the distraction, that's for sure.

Her vision blurred only slightly as the feeling of exaltation and happiness she'd felt since waking up in Sam's hotel room started to dissipate, replaced by a wave of tiredness and a headache.

Perhaps, I just need another cup of coffee...

Or perhaps, it has to do with the vampire who showed up once again out of nowhere to drive you fucking crazy.

Ava let out a sigh as she bit off

another piece of dessert.

Of all the things to happen in the middle of Oklahoma, *he* had the audacity to show up and *claim* he hadn't followed her. As if she would believe his pleas.

Vampires lie.

It's what they do.

It's how they're programmed.

Say whatever they need to, to get you alone, to get their fangs in you, and call it a day.

Yet, she'd gone willingly with a *known* vampire—the very one who'd marked her blood as his—regardless of knowing this.

Why?

What the hell is wrong with me?

God, it's like I'm not even myself anymore...

She closed her eyes and took a deep

breath as a wave of heat overcame her. She felt as if she was clearly losing her mind. In the two years she'd known Cas, he'd always been reserved. Yet, something about the glassy look in his eye, the way he seemed *loose*, less inhibited...

She could not deny that it was most intriguing. If she'd had any sense, she'd follow along until his guard was down completely, until he wouldn't suspect a thing, and then she'd put a stake through his chest, just like all the other vampires she'd come to slay since that fateful day in the frat house basement, where they'd first met.

Yet, she could not rationalize such actions when he smiled as he did, exposing a hint of fangs. When he smirked at her, eating his prize donut like a king on a throne. When he held the umbrella over her head, not even blinking as he stood drenched in the rain.

He's been gone awhile...

Ava's phone vibrated in her pocket, pulling her from her thoughts. Sliding it out, the lit-up screen displayed a text message. It was her brother.

Team meeting in my hotel room in ten minutes.

Be there.

"Cryptic and dramatic, as always," she grumbled as she set the phone down on the table, just as Cassius returned, looking as stoic and gorgeous as ever.

Why does he always have to look so fucking pretty?

Just once I'd love to see him have a bad hair day or something...

"I was starting to think you'd bailed on me." Ava sat back against the booth, gazing up at him, taking in all the fine details of the immortal creature in front of her.

His bright green eyes sparkled in the light, soft shadows falling across his pale skin from his golden hair, which was still slightly damp and pushed back to show his angelic features. His perfect jaw, smooth cheekbones.

"A gentleman never leaves his date unattended for long," he said with a smile that exposed just a hint of fang.

Ava's skin prickled with goosebumps, her wrist flaring with heat the way it always did when he was around. When she was around *vampires* in general.

"Well, good thing you're not a gentleman and this isn't a date," she said the words plainly, and did not miss the slight furrow of his eyebrows. It wasn't a date. After all, a date was something you did with someone you liked.

Ava didn't *like* Cas. Not like *that*. He was sexy and mysterious, yes, but he wasn't *alive*, and she certainly didn't trust him as far as she could throw him, and yet...

Before she could speak, or completely process such a thought, the waitress dropped off a box, and Ava started filling it with the leftover donuts as Cassius reached for his wallet.

"I got it, Cas." Her voice was solid.

"My idea, my treat." He smiled at her, as if nothing had happened. As if the man who'd left for the bathroom and the one who returned were two entirely different people. She twisted her lips into a wry expression.

Did I miss something?

"Really…" she started, but he waved her off and handed a wad of bills to the waitress.

"Keep the change," he spoke clearly, politely.

Ava glanced at him with suspicion once more but closed the box as the waitress nodded and sauntered off, leaving the two of them once again at odds.

"You didn't have to do that," she said, sliding out of the booth with the box in her hands.

"I know. But I wanted to…" The words made Ava uncomfortable and she averted her gaze.

"Well, thanks. I guess."

"You are quite welcome," he said as he rose from the booth and came to stand in front of her.

"I, uh... wish I could stay, but... Mal texted me, wants to meet up."

Cassius looked as if he was struggling with something, his eyes dancing back and forth nervously.

Ava moved to turn, his voice stopping her.

"Would you like some company along the way?" He looked into her eyes, and in them she saw something she hadn't expected to see.

Hope.

Don't be ridiculous Ava, he just wants your blood.

Nothing more.

He's not capable of wanting anything else.

Her brain battled with the twisting butterflies in her stomach and the feeling of guilt. Though, why leaving a vampire alone in a donut shop would make her feel guilty, she was uncertain. It didn't make sense. Then again, lately nothing was making sense, and it was as if the world was upside down. So, instead of spouting an angry remark or sarcastic comment, instead of turning heel and leaving him in the dust, she found herself going against the grain, against what she knew she *should* do.

"Okay." Her answer was short, but it was enough to make Cassius's lips turn up ever so slightly in the corner.

***

Ava set the box of donuts down lightly on the bureau, sat on the edge of her bed, and only then did she finally let out a deep sigh. Her head was pounding, and she felt slightly queasy, like she felt when hungover. Except, Ava knew the alcohol she'd consumed at Hamlet's was out of her system by now.

Perhaps, I shouldn't have eaten four donuts in one sitting.

That was probably not a good decision.

She fell back on her hotel bed, looking at the ceiling as the events of the past forty-eight hours hit her. She let her hand fall to her chest, feeling the beat of her heart as she closed her eyes.

Meeting Sam in Hamlet's.

The first night they'd spent together; exploring one another.

Tasting each other.

The vampire who attacked Vinny and

then her.

Dallas's arms holding her tight.

Waking up snuggled against his solid, warm chest.

Sam's sexy smile at the panel.

Cassius shielding her from the rain.

His fangs tearing into a donut, all but ripping it to shreds with that sexy, victorious smile.

Her impending date with the sexy celebrity demonologist.

She'd come to TerrorCon to relax, to enjoy a celebration of movies and fandom, but yet she had barely made it to any panels, or met anyone aside from Sam.

"That's it! After your date tonight, it's panels and movies! No more of this fucking around!" she chastised herself.

"You need to focus on the important

things," she whispered aloud, her fingers running over her raised scar on her wrist.

The important things.

Finding a way to remove Cas's mark.

Finding the vampires responsible for killing her parents.

Her phone vibrated against her hip, and she sighed, knowing exactly who it was.

"I'm coming," she said as she forced herself up off the bed, grabbing her skull clutch and heading next door to Mal's room for the impromptu meeting with renewed focus.

CHAPTER TWENTY-SIX

AVA KNOCKED ON the door, tapping out the beat of "The Final Countdown" like she used to do when she was little, wanting to get into her brother's room to play with his Legos. Though they hadn't said anything about it in ages, it had become a sort of language for them both. Even after moving in with their Aunt

Becky, the elaborate knock was something that brought both of them comfort.

The door opened to reveal Vinny on the other side, and Ava could see Mal sat on the edge of his bed, next to Dallas, looking a little worse for wear. Dark circles under his eyes indicated he hadn't slept well, and his pallor was slightly paler than usual.

"The prodigal son returns," she drawled as she entered the room, brushing past Vinny's flannel sleeve.

"Glad to know you were so worried about me," he grumbled, raking his hand through his hair.

"Dallas said it wasn't all that abnormal for you to be gone awhile."

Malcolm shot Dallas an annoyed glare, but Dallas didn't react. Just stood against the wall by the bed, his large arms crossed over his chest, leaning like he was over everything.

The vampires, the convention.

Mal's sudden emergence.

"Did he, now?"

"I mean, it wouldn't be the first time you stayed out past your bedtime." Dallas shrugged, avoiding Ava's gaze.

She pulled out the chair in front of the desk across from Mal, flipping it around so her legs straddled the back, her arms resting across the back languidly.

"Normally, I'd agree with you, but I wasn't gone because I wanted to be."

Tito and Hunter were camped out against the air conditioner, both looking to be eating from a large bag of barbecue chips.

"What do you mean?" Hunter asked through a mouthful of chips.

"I was abducted by a fucking Succubus."

Ava felt her blood run cold.

Cas mentioned something about Succubi and Incubi...

Maybe he was telling the truth...

"How do you know it was a Succubus?" Vinny asked.

"Well, honestly, she *seemed* normal enough, and I thought everything was kosher until we started getting our clothes off and—"

"Spare me the dirty details, please..." Ava shuddered.

"I thought I saw her eyes flash red. I just figured it was a trick of the light, but then... when she was... um... going down, her tongue felt... different. I tried to open my eyes, but everything was blurry, and I felt like a... *need* to..."

Ava twisted in her seat, uncomfortably.

"She called me *meum delicium.*"

Ava felt her heart stop, felt her blood chill.

No, that has to be a coincidence...

"My pleasure," she whispered.

"Yeah, how do you know that?" Dallas asked, his eyes settling on her.

Ava met his gaze. Though a part of her knew she should come forward, another told her not to divulge her secrets just yet. She needed to be sure first, before throwing around an accusation like that.

Just the thought, *Sam Kingsley is an Incubus* sounded too outlandish, too far-fetched.

But those words...

What were the odds the Succubus would use the same phrase the demonologist had when he was deep within her walls, pushing her over the edge?

"I mean, you can learn a lot of things if you go to college, you know," she bit back at Dallas. He regarded her a moment longer, as if contemplating the truth in her words, but when he looked away, she knew he had bought it.

"You didn't..." Tito asked cautiously.

Mal shook his head.

"No, I didn't. When she said those words, something just... something clicked. I remembered that job we worked a couple years ago, the one in Vermont. Where we went to investigate that lead... which turned out to be nothing?"

Mal's gaze danced around the room, and Ava got the feeling there was something he was implying, some code of secrecy among them that she was not sworn in on, and that made her angry.

Why would Mal keep something from her?

Especially if it was so important, he couldn't say it out loud in a private hotel room?

The hunters exchanged glances, silent nods in agreement.

"Yeah, we stumbled upon that Succubi den by accident, when we saved that guy we thought was vamp chow."

Mal nodded in agreement.

"I remembered hearing those words. Remember their significance."

"What significance?" Ava asked, and

they all turned to her, as if remembering she was there.

"The words are like... like hypnotizing. You know how magicians will hypnotize you to do something when they say a certain word, then snap their fingers and you're awake? But the minute they say that word—"

"Boom. You don't know what hit you and you do whatever they ask." Hunter clapped his hands together.

Ava swallowed nervously.

"It's like a spell they put you under to make you more pliable so they can get what they need to become an Incubus."

"How did you get out?" Tito asked as he popped a potato chip in his mouth.

"I fought my way out, of course, and when I managed to get a knife in that bitch's chest, I took whatever blood I could for anti-venom, just in case we need it, and I fucking ran out of there as fast as I could to warn you all, but I was still intoxicated. I mean, we fooled around quite a bit before she—"

"Seriously, stop. I think I'm going to throw up," Ava grumbled. It wasn't a complete lie. Her stomach seemed to be in knots.

"So we've got a vampire blood den and a Succubi den, and probably an Incubus floating around somewhere where there's a massive concentration of humans?" Vinny sighed.

"Yeah, and I think those fucking demons are the ones responsible for the murders."

"And how do you figure that?" Ava asked skeptically.

"I heard them talking, when I was

trying to escape. They're planning some kind of attack at The Dark Hearts Club in the dungeon, where all the bloodsuckers are going to be."

"So, they're after the vampires?" Tito asked curiously.

"No." Ava shook her head, Cas's words finally making sense.

"No, I think they want the den. For breeding grounds. A vampire owns it, so it only makes sense they'd try to squeeze them out."

Dallas twisted his lips, his gaze heated as it fell on her.

"And how do you know that?"

"Call it a really good hunch," she said as she stared back at him.

"Ava's right. It's the perfect motive. How many people visit a strip club on a daily basis? There's enough lust in one of those places to keep an Incubus or Succubus *rolling* in human ass for eternity."

"We have to stop them," Mal said definitively.

Dallas looked at Mal, nodding in response. The other hunters did the same. Then, they all turned to her.

"What are you looking at me for?"

"Are you in or are you out, Ava?" Mal asked.

Ava felt on the edge of a cliff, as if she was being pressed to jump. To jump into uncertainty and potentially wind up vampire chow or worse, an incubator for a demon spawn. Yet, the predator advancing on her would surely take her under if she did not jump.

She wanted to say no. To walk away and let the Succubi take out the vampires, to let it all dissolve into dark matter, far, far away from her. But she knew deep down in the depths of her soul that she would not be able to turn away.

The lives they could save if they worked together...

They could take out a den and a nest, and it would be a hell of a win, and Ava was always good at calling the winning horse.

"I'm in," she said.

"But you should know I have a date tonight."

Mal rolled his eyes. "Of course you do."

"With Sam?" Vinny raised his eyebrow, a soft smile playing at his lips.

"As a matter of fact, yes. We're going to dinner around seven." Ava smiled, her nerves alighting at the mention of his name. If he truly was what she did not want to say, she'd find out tonight. She had to know, and there was only one way to truly find out. She'd gotten up close and personal with vampires quite often, right before she delivered the blowing kill.

"Maybe it's better that she doesn't come. I mean, it'd be one less person to worry about," Dallas grumbled. The tone, the way he averted his gaze, and his words ignited a fire within Ava that stoked her dormant rage.

Who the hell do you think you are, Jake?

"Dallas has a point..." Tito added.

"Who says I can't find time to dine and slay?" she bit.

Mal chuckled, rolling his eyes.

"I mean, he's not wrong, but we can always use backup if you think you can handle it." Mal smiled at her, and in his eyes, she could see he had faith, trusted her to watch his back and everyone else's. She also knew her brother well enough that he would prefer to keep her in his line of sight for peace of mind, rather than out of it.

"Please. You had me at the den of vamps."

"Think you can get your demonologist date to bring you to The DHC?" Mal raised an eyebrow.

"I think I can manage that," Ava responded solidly.

"Good. Get some rest, guys, because tonight we're going hunting."

CHAPTER TWENTY-SEVEN

LEBLANC'S WAS LIKE stepping back in time. From the ornate woodwork and marbled tile to the art deco-frosted glass and framed prints on the wall. In the historic town of Ansley, it screamed opulence.

Cassius sipped his Bordeaux anxiously. Of course, Cora would pick this place.

She'd lived under Leon's roof long enough to form an attachment to all things decadent and luxurious, not to mention she didn't know Cassius's history. She only knew what had been visible to her over the decades, and his relationship with Eden was off the table of knowledge.

"It does not have to be this way, Eden. You do not have to shut me out."

"How noble of you to come to my rescue," she drawled.

"You and I both know this arrangement is what is best, given our circumstances." Cassius reached across the table, his fingers brushing the top of Eden's hand. She pulled away, setting it in her lap.

"Is that all I am to you? A

circumstance?" Her dark eyes were vacant, no glimmer of life in them. No hope, no sadness, just empty pools.

"Of course not. How can you say that after I—"

"After you what? Rode in on your white horse to sweep poor damsel Edie off her feet? Oh, what would I have done without you, my dear Cassius?" she mocked, her eyes grazing over the form of a young busboy who had his arms stacked with dishes.

"I am a victim, too, you know!" Cassius grumbled, leaving his hand on the open table.

Eden licked her lips as the young man hefted his dishes through the kitchen doors, her gaze settling at his backside.

"A victim of what? You are not the one riddled with the pressure of delivering an *heir. A perfect heir, might I add."*

"I am your victim, Edie. Every day I fight for your attention, fight to try and make this arrangement more than something we have to do. I threw myself on the fire for you, and you won't even fucking look at me."

Eden's eyes shifted to Cassius, taking in the sight of him.

"If you just give this a chance, a real chance..."

"We both agreed to uphold this engagement. You said so yourself, feelings would be left off the table." She grabbed her glass of wine, fingernails scratching the glass.

"Because I did not want to rush you. You had just lost Marcellus..."

Shattered glass rained over the table, across her lap, red wine bleeding onto the fresh white linens, spreading quickly.

"Don't say his name."

"I cannot keep on like this. Competing with a ghost."

"Then don't. I am not forcing you to stay."

Her words were true, but yet, they were not. She was not forcing him to stay, but his duty to uphold the agreement, the agreement that kept his mother protected and safe, was of the utmost importance. If he left, surely the agreement would end. He'd do whatever it took to make sure those he loved were taken care of. Though, at the time, it hadn't seemed like such a miserable sentence. He'd been hopeful that perhaps in the ashes of Marcellus's death, in the space between their friendship, perhaps, they could be more.

Despite being an engagement of convenience and breeding, Cassius hoped they could build some semblance of a life together. Yet, that life was an uphill battle wrought with thorns and storms that would not relent, would not cease to give Cassius one breath of serenity.

"Can you look at me and honestly say you wish me to go?" His voice was strained, full of remorse, pain.

Eden rose from her seat, gazing down at Cassius like a vengeful goddess ready to strike her killing blow.

"I will make this simple for you, then." She sauntered closer, trailing her long fingers along his jaw, lifting his chin with her pointer finger.

Cassius looked up at her, taking in the sight of her beauty. The scent of vanilla and roses filled the air once more.

Thrall.

Eden's thrall seeped around him like a blanketing fog, and his cock hardened at her touch, his pupils dilating. He found himself unable to move and that both alarmed him and excited him all the same.

"I belong to no one. Not you, not Francesca, not the damn High Covens."

Her fingers traced his neck, nails dragging over the veins softly, before they gripped his neck tighter. Not tight enough he couldn't breathe, but tight enough to imply the seriousness of her words.

"You cannot have my heart, Cassius," she whispered as her thrall sank deep into his bones, into his brain, taking over.

It was an almost heavenly feeling, except for the fact he could not move of *his own accord, something that left him feeling alarmed. Her words left a sadness, an ache in his chest, and she looked at him with a spark of interest, and in her eyes, he could see his own fear.*

She'd never exuded her thrall on him before.

"But my body is yours to take, should you decide to put your emotional agony aside. Now, I am done with this dinner and this conversation."

Cora prattled on about the menu, her bright pink lips moving a mile a minute.

"I know circumstances could be better, but I am truly glad you came," she said sweetly, folding her hands in her lap.

She looked stunning against the luxurious setting, her bright red hair falling over her shoulders in long curls, parts of it in the front had been pulled back to frame her heart-shaped face. She'd always been a beautiful girl, no matter the fashions of the decade.

"Yes, well, Leon's done much for me over the years, it was only right I return the favor."

"Why did you leave the house?" she asked and then took a sip of her water.

"Too many memories. Not all of them are good ones."

Cora nodded in agreement. "I get it. Still wish you could have stayed. I liked having someone else in the house for once. Someone I know."

Cassius ran his fingers around the base of his wine glass, debating his words. With the toxin out of his system, he was finally able to think clearly, process everything he'd learned.

The more he thought about Ava's words, the more it made sense. If they truly didn't look any different than the average human mortal, plenty of them could have already infiltrated the club. He decided to take a chance.

"I believe I may have a lead on the situation with Leon."

"Oh really?" She tore into a piece of bread, dredging it around on the plate of olive oil between them.

"It is Succubi and Incubi mating season, you know."

Cora did not flinch at his words. "Yeah, I know."

How interesting...

"How do you know about that?"

"Well, there's this guy who's been filming a documentary in the area. Sam

Kingsley, I think is his name. Anyway, he's making some kind of 'vampire tell all' and has been filming at the club for a while, and I overheard him talking to someone on his crew about working a case that turned out to be a Succubus, where they only come out every so many years when it's 'mating season.' Guess he's like, some big demon exorciser or something." She shrugged. A couple passed them, and Cassius did not break his gaze from Cora.

"How does Leon feel about this documentary?"

"He's been a bit of a stickler about it. You know Leon. Loves information but doesn't always want people to have it. Likes being the smartest guy in the room."

"You didn't think *any* of this was

pertinent information?" Cassius pursed his lips, feeling agitated.

"Not really. I mean, the documentary has nothing to do with the murder accusations, and Succubi are harmless to us. It's not like they pose a threat or anything."

"How long have you been locked up in that mansion?" Cassius huffed. "Of course they pose a threat. They are demons, Cora."

"Yeah, and who's to say we aren't the very same thing?"

"We are *not* creatures from Hell." His voice only rose an octave.

"We feed on blood and sex just the same."

"They feed on *lust*. Their only function is to overtake a host and spread their seed. That's it. One goal. We are more than what we feast on. We are more than our hunger for blood and our libidos."

"They are just doing what is natural for them! None of them asked to awaken during the mating season! They're just trying to make sense of what they are, the same way we are."

"I cannot believe you are defending them. They are likely responsible for *murders*. The very ones that Leon has been accused of!"

Cora huffed indignantly.

"And you are not? I remember you have killed your fair share of mortals in your day."

"That was different, Cora, and you know that. And furthermore, I have never taken pleasure in what I have had to do to survive."

"I do not wish to argue with you, Cassius," Cora said, crossing her arms.

"We are not arguing. We are having a discussion."

"Well, I do not like this discussion or your insinuations. We can agree to disagree, can we not?"

Cassius weighed her words. She'd been careless in her regard to tell him everything, and such a thing did leave him feeling perturbed. But she did have a very good point. While he was adamant they were different from the demon spawn, he could not help but see the similarities, and seeing Cora passionately defend them, even if she shouldn't... made him slightly proud. It would appear Leon's teachings had taken, after all. He did not like her insinuations, either, but he knew he needed to keep a clear head.

He also knew he needed access to the blood den. If Ava was right and the Succubi were there... he needed to find out. He needed to gather his evidence and be a hundred percent certain before going to Leon with his findings.

"I do not wish to argue with you, either. We will table this discussion. For now, but it is far from over."

He brought the glass of wine to his lips and took a long drink as another couple passed by, heading to their table, and a familiar scent filled his nostrils.

Jasmine and bergamot.

Cassius set his glass down, snapping his head in the direction they'd walked.

No, it can't be...

His gaze settled on long, pale legs that left his throat dry, and made the throbbing pulse in his veins ebb like a sonar. His gaze traveled upward, settling on the sway of the hips said legs belonged to, onto the curves he knew all too well. And when she turned around, looking over her shoulder—amber eyes ablaze—Cassius did not look away.

CHAPTER TWENTY-EIGHT

THE LAST PERSON Ava expected to see at Le Blanc's on her date with Sam was the redheaded vampire who'd attacked Vinny. Sitting with Cassius, of all people.

Who is she?

Ava felt awash with hunger, jealousy.

What the hell is she doing with Cas?

A part of her wanted to stake the

beautiful creature, right here in the middle of the room, but she knew better than to draw attention to herself in a public setting. Having to explain to a room full of people that you'd just killed a vampire didn't always go over well, as most people didn't know vampires even existed. Not unless you were thrust into the world of blood and ash the way she or Mal, Dallas, or even Sam had been. No, if she staked this woman making eyes at Cassius, she'd only look like a psychopath.

Sam slid into the open booth, and Ava followed suit. The man really did clean up nicely. Even on the show, he was quite casual, wearing nothing but band tees and horror-centric shirts and jeans, despite being in his thirties. Yet, when she'd met him in the lobby at six-thirty as directed, she'd hardly recognized him, dressed in a well-tailored gray suit with a stark-red tie.

Ava hadn't planned on fancy dinners with her brother and, therefore, was pressed for something to wear that could pass as appropriate for a date. She'd settled on the long, form fitting black dress she'd brought for her *Elvira: Mistress of the Dark* cosplay. By the look on Sam's face upon her entrance, he did not mind one bit.

Sam leaned in close to her, setting his hand on her exposed thigh.

"I'm really glad you showed up. I was worried I was going to have to dine alone again."

"Well, one thing you should know about me is that the way to my heart is through my stomach."

"I will remember that," he said with a light squeeze as he picked up his menu.

So far so good, he doesn't suspect I know anything, which is good.

"How was your panel?" she asked, attempting to make small talk. The realization they hadn't spoken much made her anxious, and it was as if she was clear of mind for the first time in days. With her wits about her, she was acutely aware of all the visible flaws between her and the attractive man next to her.

"It was all right. It was just a basic Demonology 101 panel with Kristen."

"Your co-host. Yeah, I haven't really seen much of her during the con."

"She hates these things, so she's usually holed up in her hotel room any time she's not on the clock." Sam air-quoted his last words, and Ava couldn't help her smile.

She started to feel slightly at ease, but nevertheless, the edge was still there. She could feel a fiery gaze from across the room and she didn't have to look to know where it was coming from. Her wrist flared with heat and her skin prickled with goosebumps under her long black sleeves.

"I know you don't like to talk about work, but I did have some questions I was hoping I could pick your brain about?" She crossed her legs, angling herself toward him, the motion pushing her breasts together, all but popping out in the space between her plunging neckline.

Sam's gaze dipped to her cleavage, his tongue flicking out over his lips. The lights dimmed, and for a moment Ava could have sworn she saw a flash of red in his eyes, but when he looked back up at her there was no evidence. No red eyes, no shimmer or glow, but once she got him alone in the den... she'd know for sure. Still, she needed to act as if nothing had changed, for if he was truly an Incubus as she suspected, he would be dying to close the deal, the ritual tonight.

I really do need to get a grip on myself.

"Sure, shoot."

"I um... kind of have a secret. I don't normally tell people this but—" She leaned closer, settling her hand on his thigh, rubbing slightly. The need to touch him, to feel him was becoming difficult to fight the closer she was, and when his sweet, fiery scent surrounded her she couldn't help but give in.

She traipsed her fingers up his thigh, resting them just alongside his groin.

"And you want to share it with me? I'm flattered," he said with a smile, placing his hand on top of hers.

The touch, even as faint as it was, stirred butterflies in her stomach, her skin crawling with the need to feel his touch everywhere. Somewhere in her rational brain, she understood the reason, but a part of her wished it was something else. That the connection she felt with Sam was because she liked him, and not the ever-flowing toxins he secreted. She wished her attraction was beyond chemical, but when she looked into his dark, alluring eyes she knew at that moment it was both. Which made everything she was about to do, so much more difficult.

He needed to trust her.

Needed to think he had her, for her to get close to him; close enough she could exorcize the demon within him.

But it was a risky process.

Dallas would assist her; he was the hunter with the most experience exorcizing and cleansing in their little band of misfits. As long as Ava could get Sam downstairs, in the private dens, Dallas and Mal would take care of the rest, and the vampires...

The thought of sinking her stake into a fresh vamp caused her heart to skip a beat. So much had happened, and she wasn't entirely sure how to feel about any of it, but the promise that came with her stake was enough to make her forget, enough to abate the turmoil even if it didn't last.

"I know the truth. About vampires, I mean. Well, actually, I know the truth about a lot of things, but if I had to pick one line of study, it'd be vamps."

"Oh really?" Sam's eyes focused on her intently, but before Ava could speak, the waitress was at their table.

"We'll have a bottle of champagne, please, to start," he said, barely even looking at the waitress, and within minutes she had disappeared.

"Please, continue," he said as his fingers grazed her skin, his thumb brushing over her raised scar.

The touch felt... *cold.*

Like ice.

In the presence of vampires, her skin always prickled with goosebumps, but her wrist... her wrist where Cassius's fangs had marked her skin, was always *warm*. So warm, in fact, she felt as if her blood was boiling. But despite being in the same room with a vampire, she did not feel what she always did.

Instead she felt the opposite.

Chilled, cold.

Perhaps they do have a tell after all.

"Two years ago, my boyfriend... he was killed. By vamps. I saw the whole thing." It wasn't hard to feign sadness, for Ross's death would always haunt her. His moan of pleasure, right before his scream of pain as the vampire fed on him.

"Oh my God, Ava..." Sam's eyebrows furrowed, and he scooted closer, taking her hand in his free one, moving the other to around her back, pulling her close. Up close, she could smell his aftershave. She closed her eyes and breathed him in deeply. It was the most pleasant smell.

"It's... it's okay. I mean, it's not *okay,* but... anyway—I learned all about the monsters hiding in the dark that day."

Sam's fingers brushed over her scar slowly. "I wanted to ask you about this, but I didn't think it was any of my business."

His dark eyes dipped to where his fingers caressed her, and she couldn't deny the touch stirred the butterflies in her stomach once more.

"Ask away," she whispered, feeling overrun by emotion.

"Claimed by a vampire?" It was a statement more than a question, definitive. His words were heavy, and the way they made Ava feel…

Guilt, shame, anger, and sadness all pushed forth. She hadn't understood in that very moment what Cassius was asking. All she knew was she would have done anything to live.

"Yes," she whispered. "I've been searching for a way to break the bond for two years."

Sam licked his lips, his fingers splayed at her back, brushing along the edge of her hair.

"Are you scared he'll come back to finish what he started?" Sam's words were heavy in the air between them.

Ava's eyes lifted only a fraction, and she gazed at Cassius through her long lashes, watching as he gracefully sipped his drink.

Red wine.

A well aged Bordeaux, probably.

She knew how much he favored red wine, always raiding her fridge in the middle of the night when she'd awakened from a terrible nightmare. She'd always threatened to end him if he kept showing up without warning, yet, she could not close her window at night.

Her housekeeper, Connie, had even started stocking wine in the fridge more often, if only to appease Cas. She was always prattling on about him; about how perfect he was.

As if I don't already know that.

He's designed to be perfect, but I will not fall into that web of deception.

"Every day," she answered, looking away once more.

"But I'll be ready when he does. I've trained. I've learned everything I can. I don't leave home without my stakes."

"Stakes? So you are..."

"A slayer," she whispered the words and the silence between them was most palpable.

Sam pressed his lips into a thin line, a look of contemplation on his face.

"I get why you don't tell people that."

"Yeah, well, I just... I'm not saying this is going to go anywhere, but if it does... I just... I need you to know the truth."

"I remember the first time I exorcized a demon. I was fourteen. I'd been studying exorcisms and demonology for a while at that point, but I hadn't really told anyone about it. I suspected there was a crossroads demon praying on people in my town. I couldn't prove it, until my friend made a deal and wasn't able to hold up their end of the bargain."

"I'm sorry, that must have been difficult for you, being so young and all."

"Sometimes, you don't know what you're made of until you're made." A soft smile tugged at his lips as he drew her closer.

Ava looked into his deep brown eyes, and started to feel lightheaded, the desire in her stomach only spreading under his serious gaze.

"What are you made of, Sam?" she whispered, her gaze dipping to his lips, remembering how they tasted, how they felt against her own. Somewhere in her mind, she sensed danger. But that was the difference between Ava and everyone else. Most people sensed danger and they fled. Ava flirted with it, instead, dancing the tightrope just to see how far she could fall before she lost herself completely. In the presence of this man, she could not think clearly.

"I think you know by now, *meum iuvat.*"

His words were like smooth caramel over chilled vanilla ice cream, and when Ava brought her lips to his, she fell from the cliff into the abyss below. And as his lips moved hungrily against hers, a soft moan escaped her throat. He tasted like the icing of a red velvet supreme donut, and for a moment, as she closed her eyes, she let herself enjoy the taste and all the desire it stirred within her soul.

CHAPTER TWENTY-NINE

THE DARK HEARTS Club was in full force.

Cora clutched his arm tightly as they moved through the thick crowd of mortals on the top floor, the pink, purple, and blue lights roving over the crowd. There were two dancers on stage, one at each end of the catwalk. While one was crawling around on her hands and knees seductively, the other he recognized from the previous night. The blonde, who'd looked at him with her hands around her throat. She danced gracefully around the pole, the motions reminding him of a ballerina he'd once known.

Marguerite.

The one and only woman he'd ever had as a sustainable food source, in his early years with Marcellus and Octavius. Though, like most of the women Cassius had cared for in his long life, her fate did not end well.

Because of Eden and her jealousy.

Even in the days Eden fought him, she could not keep her hands clean. Spurred by the madness of her addiction to supernatural blood—witch blood, demon blood, it was all the same to her—she did not want him, but she could not stand anyone else coming close to having him, either.

I did it to protect you.

Her words were always the same, every time, but they did not change the reality of the deaths that were on his conscience, merely because of one's relationship with him, even if said relationships were platonic at best.

"Maybe we could hang out for a bit before heading downstairs? I always like to have a little fun first before I retire to my den."

"*Your* den?" Cassius raised an eyebrow in question.

"Well, of course *my* den. What do you think I do? Hunt like an animal?" She rolled her eyes.

Cassius pressed his lips in a thin line. "I am just surprised."

"You aren't the only one who dislikes spontaneous feeding or killing, Cassius. It's messy. I don't like messy."

"Do you have a... what is the word? Fox?" he asked nervously.

"I do. But I also entertain others from time to time." She stopped in the middle of the crowd, turning her body close to his, snaking her arms up around his neck.

"When was the last time you danced, Cassius?" She gazed up into his emerald eyes, searching for something from him.

Acceptance, permission.

What, he was not sure of.

He wrapped his arms around her waist, yet left space between them. A dance was just a dance, after all. It did not mean anything.

"I spent much of the late eighties and nineties working and traversing clubs."

"And since then?"

"Since then, I have kept to myself. I do not indulge. Not anymore." He scanned the room, at the bodies beside them, in front of them, of the dancers on the stage, and the waitresses and waiters dropping off drink orders. In many ways the world had changed in appearance, but at its core it was still the same, and always would be.

Cora pulled herself closer, closing the gap between them, and Cassius pushed her away only a fraction.

"This is a good distance."

"What are you afraid of? I don't bite. Much." She giggled.

"Cora..."

"Don't think, Cassius. Just… enjoy this for what it is. Stop fighting what is in your nature."

Cassius breathed deeply, and she pulled herself closer once more, letting her small fingers trail over the fabric of his black dress shirt, over the tiny plastic buttons.

"It's okay to have fun," she said as she slid her hand over his heart. "It's okay to live in the moment, without expectations or guilt. You carry too much."

Cassius moved back and forth to the rhythm, and Cora followed without question.

After a couple songs, Cora ventured to the bar for refreshment, returning with two drinks.

"What is this?" Cassius asked

skeptically.

"A cocktail," she teased as she offered him the drink.

"I know that, but what is it?" he asked as he took the glass from her hand.

"I recall your favor for sweeter things in life, so I offer you a little concoction known as a Dracula's Kiss." She twisted her lips in amusement.

Cassius sipped the dark liquid, and the tastes exploded on his tongue.

Cherry, of course.

"It is delicious." He smiled as he took another sip. Though vampirism made it difficult for him to get drunk, it was not uncommon for him to feel slightly inebriated. Though, keeping the alcoholic buzz going was not an easy feat and usually required a litany of cocktails and hours of drinking. But after nearly a bottle of red wine, and nearly half a Dracula's Kiss, Cassius was starting to feel a little more relaxed.

Cora smiled at him through her lashes, spinning the liquid around with her cocktail straw before putting it to her lips and sucking. She watched him carefully as the lights and music shifted, signaling the change in dancers.

He drained the rest of his drink almost instantly, savoring the sweet taste on his tongue before biting into the candied cherries at the bottom just as the speakers came on to announce the next set of dancers.

Cora grabbed his drink from his hands before leaving him to dispose of their glasses, and he had to admit it did feel good to just... dance. To just be in the moment, for the moment, carefree. He'd venture down to the den soon enough, and it would all disappear.

"Please welcome to the stage, Avarice!"

Well, that certainly isn't a name you hear every day...

The dark guitar riffs of "Sweet Dreams" filled the air, but it wasn't the version he was familiar with from living during the era of the Eurythmics. No, this one had a deep, male voice crooning about "some of them want to use you..."

And when Cassius turned to get a look at the new dancer, he gasped in surprise.

Perhaps, Cora has spiked my drink and I am hallucinating.

For the second time in twenty-four hours, Cassius was battling with whether or not he was surely going insane.

My sweet Avarice...

Ava sauntered down the catwalk, all long legs and curves, just the way Cassius had always dreamed about. He was only half certain he was dreaming, as if somehow the Succubi toxin had leeched its way into his brain and brought forth an image directly from his fantasies.

Though, she was still much more clothed than the previous dancers, wearing her long, skintight black dress she'd worn to dinner with the man she was with.

Is he here as well?

Surely...

The high slit in her dress accentuated her slender legs and when she moved, the movements were deliberate and confident. When she made her way to the pole at the end of the catwalk, he waited with bated breath to see what she'd do. For once, he was glad to be anonymous, lost in the sea of people.

She did not waste a moment as she circled it, arching her arms behind her, grasping onto the steel. She pointed her toes and arched her back, the motion rather graceful, but somehow more appealing than anything he'd witnessed in The Dark Hearts Club, yet.

His gaze trailed over the curve of her spine, dipping farther down, following her movement as she slid down the pole. Her eyes fluttered, she bit her lip, and his throat went dry. The overwhelming *need* for release hit him like a ton of bricks, and he found it hard to breathe.

"Someone looks hungry." Cora's tiny fingers slid across his chest as she came up behind him, her voice hazy with lust.

Lust...

Didn't I come here for...

A wave of euphoria washed over Cassius, and he moved to shift his erection.

"I see the toxins taking effect." Cora giggled as her hands slid over top of the waistband of his pants. She turned him toward her, breaking his gaze for only a moment as her words registered.

"What did you say?" he breathed darkly. His vision blurred, and he could see her pupils had dilated."

"I think it's time we head downstairs, Cassius," she whispered as she snaked her arms up his chest, her fingers pulling him by the neck down toward her.

Alarm bells sounded all throughout his brain as Cora's thrall wrapped around him like a snake.

The euphoria.

The drink.

Her thrall.

It all felt too similar, like history was repeating itself.

"No one fights like you do, Cassius," Eden purred in his ear as her fingernails dragged across his bare chest, eliciting tiny slivers of black blood from his pale skin.

"Not everything has to be a fight, Edie," he said as he claimed her lips with his own.

The toxins from the Succubus they'd consumed were in full effect. Where there should have been pain, there was only pleasure, and the maddening desire to bury himself inside of Eden until there was nothing left.

"Cora, I—"

His words were soon cut off by a searing kiss, a wet, warm tongue forcing its way in his mouth.

But it didn't feel right.

Didn't taste right.

The music thumped loudly, vibrating his being.

This was wrong.

All sorts of wrong.

He brought his hands up, placing them on Cora's chest and he *shoved* her away.

"No."

"Cassius..." she groaned, reaching out for his hands.

His head was splitting, and the world

was foggy. His cock ached for release and his throat was drier than the desert, and he was angry.

So very angry.

Cora had drugged him.

Intentionally.

He'd trusted her, and she had betrayed that trust.

Didn't she understand?

"No means no, Cora," he growled as he turned away from the crowd, anger running through him like electricity.

"Wh... Where are you going?" she mewled.

"Do not follow me," he snapped.

"Cassius, wait! I can explain!"

Cassius slid up to the bar, catching sight of RJ.

"What it'll be?" he asked, chewing his toothpick.

"I'd like to go down to the lower level."

"I told you, you're going to have to talk with Louie."

"Then get me Louie." Cassius could feel his anger spreading, no doubt elevated by the toxin in his blood.

"Well, well, if it isn't a giant pain in my ass," a familiar voice sounded next to him.

"Hello, Malcolm." Cassius tried his best to still his building fury as he turned to see familiar brown eyes and shaggy dark hair.

"Cassius. Should have known you'd follow my sister across state lines."

"I am not here for your sister."

"Good. Then I don't have to tell you if you touch her, I will kill you."

"Your threats are wasted. I would never hurt Ava."

"You already did, the day you bit her."

Cassius's blood boiled like an overflowing pot on the stove, and he ran his shaking hand through his hair.

"I saved her life." His words rattled in the space between them, and in a flash he was closer to Mal than he'd ever been, and though he should have remained cool, he was at his wit's end. With Mal's callous demeanor, Ava and her hot and cold attitude, with Cora and her disrespect for boundaries, with the Succubi who were throwing a monkey wrench in the whole ordeal.

So he did not remain cool.

No.

He bared his fangs to Malcolm Reynolds, in the shadows of The Dark Hearts Club.

"And I would do it again."

"If you know what's good for you, *Cas*—"

Hearing Malcolm use the nickname Ava had given him made him feel all sorts of emotions.

"You'll do as I say and leave. Stay the fuck away from this place tonight."

"Why is that?"

"Because this place is going to go down in flames," Mal said as he drained the last of his drink, turning away from the bar, the lights catching on the gleam of his blessed silver blade.

His words were serious.

Was he *warning* him?

Was he insinuating he was going to...

Cassius did not want to finish the thought, as a mass killing of vampires made him sick to the stomach. Of course, the toxins would also be partially to blame.

"You would not burn down a building with your sister in it."

"Cas, my sister's gonna light the match."

CHAPTER THIRTY

AVA WAS CERTAIN of two things as she walked into The Dark Hearts Club.

The first, as her wrist flared with heat and her skin chilled upon entrance—somehow it was magnified—was that the place was crawling with vampires. Her entire being felt like a divining rod, her nerves standing at full attention. The second, was that Sam Kingsley was truly what she feared him to be.

An Incubus.

A creature of lust whose only design was to spread his poison to an unsuspecting victim. The way she felt in his presence, the maddening *need* for him to touch her, to get him alone, to let him possess her from the inside out...

She knew better, now. Those feelings didn't belong to her, they were a reaction to his power, his toxin. Toxin she'd allowed into her body more than once.

In the few hours before her date, after Vinny and Hunter had left, Ava spent what little time she had learning about the demon spawn from Tito and Mal. When Tito had left, she'd come clean: the knowledge and similarities to Mal's story too much to pass off as coincidence. To her surprise, neither of them jumped down her throat or were condescending, though, the dark look in Dallas's eyes was not one she'd soon forget. Instead, they'd only nodded in understanding, forming a plan to put an end to the demons, while trying to keep casualties to a minimum.

The mating rituals of both the Succubi and the Incubi were very different. For the ritual to culminate and impregnation to occur, the Incubus's victim needed two things. Their blood and their semen, at which point at that stage in the mating ritual, the female would have likely built a tolerance to the toxin and the chant, and submission would be a slice of cake, their willingness to feed the Incubus something more than desire. It would be *needed.*

Just the thought made Ava shiver.

Gross.

If things were going to go as planned, all she had to do was get close enough to attempt an exorcism, and avoid drinking Sam's blood, avoid his *toxin*. Yet, she looked at Sam in the light of the club, bathed in the glow of the neon, she was also certain that she'd let herself fall too far into the fantasy, and reality was a bitch.

Believing someone like him could really be interested in someone like her, how had she ever entertained such an idea?

It was outlandish, at best, and she knew, now, that he'd managed to tap into her darkest desires.

To be *wanted.*

To be worshipped and adored.

A part of her hated that she wanted such things to begin with. Life was more than finding some guy to shack up with and have a couple kids. For a brief moment, she'd thought that what she and Sam had could have been something.

Something real.

But it was all toxic lies.

It had been a sheer stroke of genius that as Ava made her way back from the bathrooms, the stage manager mistook her for someone else. Never one to back down from a challenge, a part of her understood the need for an Incubus to feed on lust; she would play the part. She would dangle herself like a carrot and be exactly what he wanted.

Meum delicium; my pleasure.

What was more lustful than watching your mate avail themselves to a roomful of spectators?

It'll definitely make a good story to tell later when all this is said and done.

As she sauntered to the edge of the catwalk, sliding down the pole like her life depended on it, she looked out into the crowd in search of Sam, but it was not his eyes she found.

Instead, she locked eyes with glowing green emeralds.

Cassius stood in the middle of the crowd, his golden hair falling, casting shadows over his perfect, angelic face. He was still dressed in his signature gray shirt and leather pants and the redheaded vamp pressed herself tightly against him, his hands around her waist. Her pulse throbbed, her heartbeat quickening.

The sight stirred a mixture of feelings within her, dancing with the Incubi toxin, a dangerous waltz.

The way he held her, his fingers against the small of her back.

The way he looked at her, and then...

Ava's heart twisted as she watched the redheaded vamp pull Cassius to her, locking lips with him like he was some leading man in a romantic movie and they were not in a crowded room. It was like time stood still, and there were only the two of them, the neon lights dancing over them like laser beams.

She was not prepared for the flurry of anger, the pang of jealousy that pushed forth, the way it heated her blood. Her fingers twitched, and she silently prayed the vampire would meet her end at her stake.

But why do I care what he does?

He isn't anything to me.

But even as she thought the thought, she knew it was a lie.

He'd claimed her blood as his, that counted for something right?

She shut down the dangerous thoughts, forcing herself to look away. Whatever fantasy she had indulged in earlier was just that.

A fantasy.

It could never be anything more.

Because one day it would come down to him or her.

And she would do whatever it took to survive, including putting a stake through his heart.

When she'd made her exit, it was not Sam who waited in the wings. Dallas stood with his arms crossed.

"Are you done playing around?" he grumbled.

"Ah, so I assume you watched the show."

"Only because I had to," he said gruffly as they walked back out toward the crowd, stopping in a shadowed alcove.

"Regardless, I think your little display worked. I saw Sam talking to the guy over by the stairs, slipping him a nice wad of cash."

"Well, then, guess my stripper skills paid off," she chortled.

"Please, Kitten. That was hardly stripping. You didn't even take your clothes off."

"Is that why you're so grouchy? Didn't get the show you wanted?" she bit as Dallas loomed over her.

"I'm *grouchy* because you're wasting my time by playing showgirl instead of taking this seriously."

"Don't tell me I'm not taking this seriously. You're not the one who got fucked by an Incubus."

Dallas's lips thinned, and a look of fury flashed in his eyes.

"Now, if you're done playing asshole, I've got a demon to entertain."

She pushed past him, searching for Sam once more. He stood by the stairs, just as Dallas had claimed, looking positively devilish. The closer she got to the stairs, the colder she felt; until she stood in front of him, a sweet smile on her face.

"You are just full of surprises aren't you, *meum delicium*?" he said darkly.

"Surprise is my middle name," she responded flirtatiously.

"I've managed to get us a private table downstairs. It's much more... intimate than those up here," Sam said as he ran his finger up and down her arm seductively.

"Isn't that where the vampires are?" She raised an eyebrow innocently.

"It is."

"Quite an invitation for a slayer. Should I be on my best behavior?" She flashed her eyelashes at him.

"In public, of course. But behind the doors of the den..." He leaned in closer, his lips brushing her ear.

"Give me your worst," he said, his eyes flickering red once more.

Cassius's words echoed in her brain.

They can only return to their true form

during the mating process.

She was counting on it.

For the minute Sam gave way to the demon that possessed him, Ava would be waiting with her crystal and holy water ready to trap the monster that claimed Sam Kingsley.

"With pleasure." Ava smiled slyly.

CHAPTER THIRTY-ONE

OUT OF THE corner of his eye, Cassius spotted Ava and her date moving down the stairs as Malcolm's words hit his ears.

Just as he noted the flash of red ghosting over her date's eyes.

His own widened in panic.

"What have you done, Malcolm?"

"I haven't done anything. Yet."

"How can you put your sister in danger consistently and not think twice about it?"

"Because if I tell her no, she'll just go in hot, and that's when you make mistakes." He shrugged, heading for the stairs.

"How do you expect to get down there?" Cassius sneered.

"Dallas already took care of that. Last chance, Cas, to get the hell outta dodge. Otherwise, I can't promise you won't end up at the end of my fucking stake."

Cassius's pulse quickened, his temper burning hotter.

"Do you know what he *is*?" he growled.

"Yeah. And so does she."

The words agitated him. Ava *knew*

the man was a demon of lust, what he was capable of, and yet there she stood on the edge of the stairs, with a wicked grin on her face. Baiting an Incubus was nothing like baiting a vampire. The two were not the same, and the way he'd looked at her...

There was no way in hell Cassius was going to leave. He'd made a vow to protect Ava the night he saved her life, and he intended to keep it.

"I am not leaving."

"It's your funeral," Malcolm said as they walked over the staircase, his pulse throbbing with every step.

True to his word, the man, Louie, took Mal's reservation and opened the velvet rope. Cassius was slightly impressed the mortal had managed an in, but he would not let him know that.

Instead, he focused on trying to fight the toxin, which was now hitting its peak. When they came to the bottom of the stairs, Cassius wondered just what he'd signed up for.

While the room upstairs was basic in its layouts and design, echoing the clubs he'd seen in the eighties, the basement level of The Dark Hearts Club looked like something straight from the pits of Hell.

Deep, crimson walls with black molding that stretched up the crevices of the walls and across the ceiling like black thorny vines, a glittering black and red crystal chandelier sparkling ruby prisms all across the black marble floor. The red velvet chaises and lounges were spread out in a circle around the stage, where the blonde-haired dancer who reminded him of Marguerite, gracefully sauntered around the stage, lit up by neon red light.

A whistle sounded next to him.

"I will give you bloodsuckers credit where it's due. Least you have style," Malcolm noted.

"What is your plan, Malcolm?" Cassius scoured the room for Ava, panic surging through him when he could not find her. There were many vampires scattered about on the lounges, some with vixens in their grasp, openly feeding while others entertained other forms of attention. Though he'd never been one for voyeurism or multiplicity, he could not deny the arousal such a sight brought him.

He shifted his stance farther from Mal, feeling quite on the spot. If the other man noticed, he didn't say anything, and for that Cassius was grateful. It was awkward enough being down here with the scent of blood and sex permeating the air, although his hunger for blood had been abated thanks to his trip to the morgue. He only had to ride out the toxin, but that was manageable—or so he told himself it was prior to setting foot in the main den.

The doors encased within the walls all bore red-lit occupied signs, and his stomach turned as the thought of Ava in one of those rooms pushed forth.

Mal slid his phone out, the light illuminating his face.

"It's showtime," he said with a smile.

The sound of a laugh cut through the air, and Cassius followed it like a beacon. There she stood, legs wrapped around the Incubus, giggling as his lips traversed the skin over her neck. But he was too late.

For as quickly as his feet picked up pace, the damage had been done, and all Cassius could do was watch as he sank his fangs into Ava Crowley, and then kissed her before whisking her away into the darkness of a locked room.

CHAPTER THIRTY-TWO

SOMETHING HAPPENED THE moment Sam's fangs pushed forth. It was as if she'd been replaced by someone else, forgetfulness now taking over. She forgot who she was, where she was. What she was supposed to be doing. In that space, instead, she had given in to her darkest desire, and let it bring her to salvation.

The thought of Sam's fangs in her neck was no longer a fantasy.

But it didn't *feel* right.

Something in the way he touched her and in the sound of his voice, she knew. Her blood rallied against the intruder, furious as her mind fought to make sense of it all.

The temperature dropped, a chill running all along her skin. She fought the fog that threatened to settle, holding on to the memories she often conjured when fighting a vampire's thrall.

But this was different.

Because it wasn't thrall she was fighting, it was her own demons.

"Your lust tastes so sweet..." Sam groaned as he pushed her up against the locked door. Her mind protested, but her body sang a different song as her hands made steady work of unbuttoning his pants, driven by lust and lust alone.

When she gazed up at him and his luscious, divine lips, his eyes flashed bright red, flickering in and out with an emerald-green glow as the demon tried to take the form of the thing she wanted most.

"I can take it away, if you let me," he whispered darkly, kissing her much more roughly than he had previously. All the other times he'd kissed her, he tasted sweet, took his time.

But now...

Now, it was as if he couldn't move fast enough, his lips falling back to her neck, sucking the blood that rushed to the surface.

And for a moment, Ava wanted to give in. Because what he promised was too difficult to say no to.

Freedom.

To end the mark.

To be free of Cassius.

To be free of the hold he had over her.

It was him who had brought her here. She'd been foolish, fallen into his net. For as much as she tried to fight it and tried to hide it, in this moment she understood what frightened her the most was that in spite of it all... he was her weakness.

Damn Cassius...

Damn this fucking bond!

"Yes," she moaned in response, sliding Sam's boxers to the floor as his hands roughly slid up her legs, her thighs, his fingers hooking into the sides of her panties, grasping at them as if they were a lifeline.

"Make it go away," she breathed as his lips pressed over her collarbone. When he pulled away, her pulse throbbed, and she felt a burning pain.

Her gaze fell on him, and she watched as his eyes shifted to a glowing solid red, as his fangs tore into his own wrist, crimson blood rushing to the surface.

And though her insides ached, her body awakening with need once more to feel him, be possessed by him...

The sight of his fangs in his own flesh ignited something within her, and lust was replaced by anger and disgust.

She needed to save this man, to exorcize the demon within him. Sam Kingsley deserved to be free, too.

She fumbled with her skull clutch, her fingers shakily grasping onto the clear quartz pillar she'd managed to fit inside.

She wasted no time as she held it to his chest, chanting the words Tito and Dallas had coached her to say.

Sam's lips turned up in the corners into a wicked smile, and his features... flickered. They shifted into someone else, something else. Where dark, inviting chocolate eyes once laid, there were pools of crimson fire; where golden skin once stood, he was now ashen gray like a stone. And he was somehow much larger, towering over her like a gargoyle instead of a man.

His fingers covered hers and he pulled the stone away with a smirk.

"Perhaps, you should stick to slaying, *meum delicium*." he hissed, his pink forked tongue sliding out of his lips. The sight made Ava want to throw up.

She'd let this *monster* into her heart?

Her body?

She shook with anger, with fear.

Oh, hell no.

"And perhaps, you should go back to Hell where you belong."

His hand nearly crushed hers as he forced her arm down, while his free hand slid up her neck, fingers tightening around her throat as the warm, sticky blood of his wrist seeped down her neck. With his tightening grip, she could feel it spreading, feel his claws in her open bite, and it hurt like hell.

"And here I thought we were on the same page." He pressed himself against her, her back aching as it meshed with the hard wall, and she could feel him and his putrid member against her thighs, wet with arousal.

She fought his hold, feeling stronger than she ever had. The toxins and adrenaline melding to give her a boost she hadn't expected. Ava brought her knee up, connecting it with his groin, and he stumbled back.

"Sorry about this, Sam... but you'll thank me later."

Screams echoed in the distance, but Ava did not flinch. She made a beeline for her crystal, spouting the chants louder, just as the door crashed in.

Dallas stood there, blade in hand, and upon hearing her chants, was at her side immediately. Combined, the Incubus started to singe, smoke billowing from his eyes and orifices.

"What the fuck took you so long?" she growled.

"There's a lot of rooms down here,

Kitten. You could've texted me."

"Oh, for the love, when would I have had time—"

Dallas hefted his body on top of the Incubus, the door swinging behind him.

"We can do this later, Ava." He straddled the Incubus by the legs, and Ava didn't miss the Incubus's flailing erection.

God I'm never going to be able to erase that from my brain.

Ava repeated the words, Dallas echoing them in tandem as she came up beside him and slammed the crystal down on his chest.

She watched as the demon before her flickered between gray skin and red eyes, back to kind brown eyes and golden skin. Watched as the gray smoke turned black, smelled the burning flesh as the crystal lit with a crimson glow.

"It's working!" Ava exclaimed, her fingers tightening around the crystal.

But just as the crystal started to fill, Ava felt a stabbing pain.

"Fuck!" She squinted her eyes, tears coming to them faster than a flood.

"Ava what's wrong…"

"It hurts…" she gasped, her neck throbbing. She shakily brought one hand up to her neck. The scent of fire and ash filled the air, and it was horrid. She felt as if she were going to be sick. Her stomach twisted, her loins aching fiercely, as if someone had taken a knife to her from the inside.

"Dallas… something's wrong… Ahhhhhh!" She clamped her legs together, curling into a ball, her fists shaking.

"Stay with it, Ava! We're almost there..."

"It burns!" she cried in agony, her vision blurring from tears and pain. She could see the steady stream of black smoke surrounding Sam Kingsley's lifeless body, and then it was over.

The smoke dissipated, filtering in a steady stream toward the crystal, and a burst of red smoke settled in its wake, like a sonic boom, edging out like a ripple on the surface of a lake, covering everything in its wake.

Ava let go of the crystal as the force blew her back into the wall.

Her entire body felt as if it were on fire, as if she was burning from the inside out.

CHAPTER THIRTY-THREE

CASSIUS FELT A pain deep within him as the scent of smoke and fire filled the air.

It all happened so quickly.

When the Incubus had shifted, he knew.

They all knew.

The Succubi couldn't deny the call of

their maker, any of which were in the proximity of him, that is. The ever-present stench of demons filled the air, and if that hadn't been enough, there was the struggle, the screams of chaos.

It was a free for all of demons, vampires, and Malcolm somewhere, likely staking those who got in his way as he collected the employees and evacuated them in the middle of the madness.

The scent of death and decay was prevalent, the putrid scent of smoke, demon expulsion, and burning flesh made his eyes water.

But none of that mattered as he felt the sting, the racing pulse in his veins.

And then he saw her.

The smoke filled the room—he could see it all spiraled into one clear crystal—

just as it glowed red and as the energy stabilized, trapping the exorcized demon in the stone, it sent a shockwave out, hitting everyone in its wake, including him.

Cassius fell back from the blast, sprawled against the floor. His chest ached from the impact, his muscles tensing immediately. The crash of toxin ebbed as he sat up, his vision blurring as he clutched his chest. The ringing in his ears subsided as he shook his head, blinking furiously.

He could withstand the pain; it was surely not the first time he'd been knocked around or fallen flat on his ass. He crawled on the floor through the red haze, below the smoke, with only one goal and one line of sight.

The sound of coughing and Ava's pain

would be etched into his brain forever, and he hated the sound. His vision cleared enough for him to see Ava against the wall, writhing in agony, screams of terror escaping her throat. "Ava?" he called in as thick smog filled his lungs, making it hard to breathe.

"Cas?" she cried, a mixture of shock and pain. The sound was like breaking glass.

He waved his hand through the smoke.

"What the fuck are you doing—" Her words dissipated in the air as another scream erupted from her.

"Make it stop!" she cried.

He hated to see her like this.

It was torture.

The Ava he knew did not cry or scream.

She fought.

To see her this way set every nerve in his body on edge. He was next to her in an instant, kneeling beside her.

Her eyes fluttered, her chest heaving with heavy breath.

"I'm here..." the words fell out of his mouth without warning as he scoured his gaze over her, trying to assess what could be causing her so much pain.

"What happened, Ava, talk to me..." He licked his lips as the sweet, divine smell of blood invaded his passageways. His fangs ached as the scent made its way throughout his senses, his cock twitching. Frustratedly, he growled at the response.

This is not the time...

Ava's head rolled to the side, her hair falling over her shoulder, and then he saw it.

Her pale neck smeared with crimson, wet, sticky blood.

His throat suddenly felt constricted, his thrall pushing forward, trying to find its way out. It was instinct, he knew that, and it was as if the world stopped. As if there was no fire, no fight.

Only him, her, and the *blood.*

Instinctively he reached out, his shaky fingers brushing along her skin, along the blood that smelled sweeter than any dessert. But there was also the scent of a demon, and he swallowed hard, trying to fight his nature.

His insides lurched with another wave of ache; panic, fear coursing through him.

He'd never known an Incubus to challenge a vampire's claim. And by the looks of things, he knew the Incubus had managed to start the ritual somehow. Given Ava was still clothed, he knew it was blood.

It would be so easy...

Venom pushed through his fangs, and his entire body felt the drive, the desire to sink his fangs into the woman he'd previously claimed. To save her, draw out the poison. To finish what he'd started two years ago, the night he'd saved her life.

Not only had the Incubus bitten her, challenged his claim, he'd spread his toxin, his blood, before he'd been exorcized from the mortal vessel's body.

No...

Not like this...

Cassius closed his eyes, pushing back against his thrall.

The world was giving him a second chance. In that moment, the one he went over in his mind time and time again, she'd said yes.

She hadn't known what that meant.

The sight of her as she cried out in pain, as she twisted on the ground, fists balled together, he knew if she were in her right mind, she'd say no and that was his last thought.

A deep coughing sound rattled in the air, pulling Cassius from his realization, and his gaze settled on another body; it was enough. Enough of a distraction that for one split second he could breathe. But it would not last long, as a force pushed him back, away from Ava, up against the wall with a knife to his throat.

"Don't touch her, you fucking tick,"

the man growled, his blue eyes full of rage.

Ava's coughs echoed in the background.

"Dallas... Sam..."

"He'll be fine, Kitten. But we need to get you out of here."

Another sharp pain shot through him from head to toe, but he pushed it aside, his fingers wrapping around the man's thick wrists.

"Ava..."

"Wait a minute, you're the vamp from the church—"

Ava coughed violently, and Cassius struggled against Dallas's hold.

"You are wasting time, she—" The way this man held him, Cassius wasn't sure he had much of a chance, but his only thought, his only worry was for the woman he loved who was struggling from the separation, the death of the Incubus who had poisoned her and started a mating ritual.

"Cassius!" Familiar voices rang out, male and female, and Cassius fought to look to where they came from.

Cora lunged for Dallas, bearing her fangs, and he swiftly changed course, swinging at Cora instead. Leon wrapped his arms around Cassius from behind, pulling him against his chest.

"Cassius, we must go..."

Cassius coughed, trying to find his breath.

"Leon, I'm sorry I—"

"It's all right, we can worry about the details later, right now we need to get out before this place goes up and takes us with it," Leon said sternly.

In the distance, he could hear Cora hissing, could hear *Dallas* slamming her up against the wall; it was white noise. All of it was white noise, because as the toxins crashed, as his mouth watered, he could feel her racing pulse in his veins.

That was what he held onto.

Malcolm stood in the doorway, covered in blood, his voice panicked.

"What did you do to her..."

"I did nothing, the Incubus, he—"

Malcolm charged Cassius, knocking Leon off of him, and within seconds his stake was against his chest.

"Malcolm, listen to me..."

"Why should I listen to a word you fucking say?" Malcolm's lips pulled back in a snarl.

"Give me one good reason why I

shouldn't dust you right here and set you on fire."

Cassius hissed, rage fueling him once more. He glanced from Malcolm and his stake pressed against his chest, to *her*.

"Ava..." Cassius's gaze fell on Ava as she stared up at him.

"She's been bitten by an Incubus," he breathed heavily, his eyes staring into her with all that he truly was.

"She needs anti-venom."

His words hit Malcolm instantly, and he watched as his expression shifted, considering his words.

"Why should I believe you?"

"If you love your sister, you can't afford not to," Cassius growled.

"Cassius, there is no time, I am sorry—"

"She bears my mark, Leon. I'm not

leaving without her."

"You're the one responsible—" Dallas shifted once more, angling himself between Leon and himself, and the sound of labored breathing and coughing; of beams breaking sounded all around them.

Dallas's fist connected with Cassius's face, once, twice, splitting his lip in the process.

The man who lay lifeless only moments ago struggled to sit up, looking dazed and confused.

"What the hell..." he coughed.

"Dallas, stop..." Ava cried as she pushed his leg, knocking him off balance. She scowled up at him as clutched at her abdomen.

"He's mine." She coughed, but her eyes were still full of fire, menacing.

"Grab her, Dallas, I have the anti-venom. If what they say is true..."

His punches stopped and Cassius broke away, seizing his chance to get away from the violence as he knelt beside Ava once more, the man—*Dallas*—arguing with Leon behind him.

"We need to get you all somewhere safe," Leon commanded.

"I'm not going anywhere with the likes of you—" Dallas growled.

"And what is your plan? To stay here and die?" Cassius asked, turning his head, angling his furious gaze at the lumbering man just as a flaming beam fell from the ceiling.

Cassius pulled Ava by the arm, just out of the way of the raining debris. She did not fight his touch, or his pull. Instead, he felt her hand on his bicep, fingers grasping on as if she was trying to ground herself, trying to push herself up...*fighting.*

Fighting to hold on, to live once more.

"The hotel will be crawling with cops. And I doubt the local emergency services will know how to treat her or..."

"Lead the way," Malcolm said, sheathing his stake.

"The fuck are you doing, Malcolm?" Dallas roared.

"Saving my sister," Malcolm yelled back as another rumble from the rafters echoed in the chamber.

"Ava, I need you to get up." Cassius focused on keeping his voice calm.

Tears streamed down her face, her eyes of fire, glassy and red rimmed. She looked back at him and nodded.

"It hurts, Cas...it hurts so fucking

bad…"

"I know, Ava, but not for much longer…"

"We must hurry." Leon nodded to Cassius.

Cassius reached out to help her stand, but Dallas pushed him aside with one large arm.

"Touch her again and you die."

Cassius knew better than to argue as the fire started to spread, the alarms ringing loudly, sprinklers spewing water like rain. He wanted to protest, wanted to tell this lumbering bag of muscle where he could shove his attitude, but he knew that would not get him anywhere.

Instead, he watched as Dallas wrapped his arms around Ava and picked her up. Her arms wrapped around his neck, her face buried in his ripped shirt. Dallas turned away from the man sitting up in the center of it all, the mortal fastening the buttons of his pants, running his hand through his hair.

As Leon led Mal, Dallas, and Ava out of the room and toward safety, Cassius had a split second to make the decision.

I could leave him here.

Leave him to disappear with this god-forsaken place...

But that was not who he was.

Cassius looked death in the eye and he said, "not today."

So, instead of turning his back and letting the flames consume the man who'd wronged his sweet Avarice, he approached the man. Cassius's gaze settled on the dark ones of the mortal man. He was delirious, confused, and scared, and Cassius did not feel anger.

Instead, he felt *compassion.*

Understanding.

After all, he's been possessed by a demon for lord knows how long...

Cassius grabbed Ava's skull purse from the floor as he made his way to the man, shoving the crystal inside, zipping it shut before reaching a hand out to the Incubus's second victim.

Though Cassius wanted to hate this man for what he'd done to Ava, he knew the man in front of him was not responsible, and so he helped him up. During this time, he let the man lean on him for support, and did not waste another second as he carried the weight of the human against him, with adrenaline fueling him.

He fled, with as much haste as he could, out of the burning Dark Hearts Club and into the shadows of the night.

Sirens bathed the street in shades of red and blue as Cassius helped the man to the nearest ambulance, and when the medic turned from him to tend to the man's wounds, Cassius disappeared into the night.

***

When Cassius walked through the doors of Leon's home, everything was different.

Cora sat on the chaise in the foyer, her hands placed delicately in her lap, looking sorrowful.

"I'm sorry, Cassius." Her voice was soft.

"You are sorry?" he scoffed as he stood just barely in the foyer. The distance between them was overwhelming.

"I did not think..."

"No, you didn't. You didn't think about anyone but yourself."

"I know that!" She sniffled, her voice shaking.

"Were there any human casualties?" The sound of his footsteps echoed in the large room.

Cora shook her head.

"Human casualties, no."

When her eyes did not meet his, he let out a deep sigh.

"And the man who'd been possessed?"

"Sam Kingsley seems to be all right. Reports say he's a bit disoriented, but he's stable."

Cassius stopped next to her, the

silence between them deafening until she spoke.

"I never meant to hurt anyone," she whispered.

"That doesn't excuse what you did."

"I know."

When Cassius entered Leon's library, he was not surprised to see him milling about with a stack of books, chewing on the arm of his glasses.

"I expected you much sooner," Leon said nonchalantly, not looking up from his book as he swayed back and forth.

Cassius's shoulders relaxed and it was as if all the world came crashing down all at once, and he held his face in his hands, a deep sigh leaving him. In the distance, he could hear the closing of the book, and within moments he felt arms around him. Warm, familiar arms, and he could not hold in the pain or emotion any longer.

"It's all right, let it out."

"No, it's not. It's a fucking disaster," he said through the first onset of tears.

Leon's hands smoothed over his arms, and the touch stirred long forgotten feelings of guilt and pain.

Even his own father had never hugged him like this.

"Your club, the murders, Ava..." His voice hung on her name, and Leon let out his own sigh.

"Why didn't you tell me, Cassius? Hmm? Why didn't you tell me you'd claimed a mate?"

"Because I thought I could handle it."

Leon let out a soft laugh, shaking his head.

"She was dying, and I... I just

couldn't leave her there. I know the repercussions of what I did. It was on Boracelli territory."

Leon held him at a distance, and Cassius wiped his eyes.

"And you thought what? You'd just fight a supernatural bond to avoid being discovered?" Leon said as he turned away, heading back to his desk.

Cassius blew out a frustrated breath.

"Something like that."

"And how's that going for you?" Leon snickered.

"Terribly." Cassius let out a shaky laugh.

"Is she...is she going to be okay?"

Leon nodded.

"Yes. I administered some anti-venom, thanks to her brother, which may take a few hours to take hold, but should do the trick. Thankfully, your mark is strong. Had it not been there, the toxins likely would have spread much quicker and we may not have made it in time."

"So, you're saying my bite..."

"Saved her life again."

Cassius blinked in shock, unsure how to process such information.

"Her fever will pitch and delirium will set in, a side effect of the anti-venom fighting off the toxin. She may say things or do things that don't make sense. Things she won't remember, but that is par for the course. Once the anti-venom is in full effect, the loopiness will taper off, and she may not remember everything fully or clearly."

Cassius processed Leon's words, unsure how to feel about them.

"And Dallas?"

"Dallas is still here, yes. He refuses to leave. Malcolm, too... You've come a long way from High Covens, haven't you, Cassius?" Leon sighed.

Cassius could not find it in him to answer and just nodded.

"Cora tried to drug me with Succubi toxin."

"She told me," Leon said as he folded his hands in front of him on his desk.

Cassius stood to the side, feeling quite tired.

"She also told me you vehemently denied her advances, even under the influence of the toxin." His tone had shifted to a much more serious one.

"Do you plan on turning the girl? Ava?"

"It is not up to me."

"You do not wish to spend immortality with her?" Leon cocked his head in surprise.

"She does not want this, and I will not force her hand."

"But if she did want this... If she came to you and asked to be bitten, would you do it?"

"In a heartbeat."

Leon crossed his legs, spinning in his chair.

"And if she never asks? How long do you think you can keep up this ruse? Vampiric Law states that you have seven years to fulfill your claim or the Boracellis can challenge you."

"I will deal with the Boracellis when the time is right. I cannot hide from them forever, I know this."

"Your father came to me one night,

much like this one. Stormy. Rainy. He came to my library in Rome and told me he'd made a mistake. In the heat of passion during his stag night, he'd bitten your mother."

"He didn't turn her for seven years, though."

"He struggled with the decision to do so as well, you know."

Cassius's eyes widened in surprise.

"Come again?"

"It was an accident. He hadn't meant to bite her, claim her. Though, he'd become quite smitten with her, and he struggled whether or not to make her his for eternity. And then he found out about you."

Cassius pursed his lips.

"If he was so smitten with her, why did he wait seven years to turn her? Why did he leave us? Why did he seek out the bed of other women if he was so *smitten* with her?" he scoffed.

"You are like him in so many ways. Smart, loyal. Stubborn."

Cassius glared at Leon, as he continued.

"Sooner or later, Cassius, you will need to make a decision."

"I know."

Leon stared at Cassius, a deafening silence falling between them.

"A word of advice?" He raised an eyebrow at Cassius, who nodded.

"Of course."

"Stay as far away from her as you can."

"Leon..."

"No, Cassius. Listen to me on this. If you do not wish to turn her or feed off of her... do not put yourself through the agony. A claiming bond is not meant to be drawn out. It is meant to be an eternal *bond*. It is meant to happen, naturally, in the blink of an eye. A bite for a bite. Your father sought out other women, sought out binges of blood to quiet the madness he felt around your mother because he thought he could deny his nature. And he couldn't. He did not win the fight. He surrendered."

Cassius looked away.

"I will never be like him, and if for one moment I think I am anything at all like him... I will have Ava put a stake through my heart."

Cassius pushed off the desk, slowly walking away.

"To deny our nature is madness. To give in is salvation." Leon's voice echoed in the cavernous room.

Cassius stopped at the doors, responding without turning around.

"My salvation is not worth the price of her choice," he said as he walked through the doors, closing them once and for all.

Cassius softly padded over to the guest room, the very one he'd been staying in before he left to stay at the Silver Starling.

Dallas lay with his back against the wall, his eyes shut. His chest rose and fell, the sound of snoring like a buzzing frequency.

Cassius quietly shifted past him, carefully pressing on the door, opening it ever so quietly. The room was dark, lit up only by moonlight pouring in through the windows.

Malcolm lay crumpled in an armchair, snoring away just as Dallas was outside. Even in the dark, he could make out the outline of her body on the bed. Slowly, he approached her side, his gaze roving over her sleeping form.

She always looked so peaceful, so beautiful when she slept. Long, full dark lashes fluttering ever so slightly in deep sleep against her porcelain skin, the way her mouth opened just the slightest, how she gripped her pillow, her hand behind it—usually holding a stake.

Curious, he lightly pushed her pillow up with his pointer finger, a soft smirk forming on his face when he saw the familiar stake curled in her fist.

It's nice to know some things never change.

As he drew his fingers back her eyes

fluttered.

She was awake.

"Cas?" she whispered groggily.

"Yes, my sweet Avarice?" he breathed. It was as if her words gave him life, not her blood.

The way she said his name was a spell he wanted to hear over and over.

"Where the hell am I?" she whispered, her eyes looking up at him with panic and fear.

His fingers trailed down her pillow, brushing the edge of her knuckles. Her skin was soft, but slightly clammy.

The fever.

"You are safe. Malcolm is just over there in the corner, and your lumberjack lapdog is just outside the door." He smirked.

Ava's lips turned up in the corners.

"Dallas didnt hurt you, did he?" she drawled, her eyelids fluttering once again.

"Thanks to your command, no. He did not."

"Mmm, good. I wouldn't want to see anyone wreck that annoyingly pretty face of yours." She hummed, and his heart skipped a beat.

"Besides, I have a claim on you," she whispered.

"Yes, you do," he whispered back.

"You're mine to slay," she whispered, looking up at him with fire and delight in her eyes.

His voice caught in his throat, and the words tumbled out of his mouth without warning.

"Yes. I am yours. Forevermore."

"I would kill for a donut, right now,

and a drink," she grumbled, and he couldn't help but smile.

"What kind?"

"Red velvet supreme," she whispered as she closed her eyes.

His fingers traced lines over her knuckles, his thumb brushing the scar on the underside of her wrist, and he could feel her pulse quicken at the touch both beneath his fingertips and in his veins.

"I thought you preferred jelly filled. Cherry, raspberry."

"Cas likes red velvet. And Bordeaux." Her fingers unfurled from their hold on her stake, splaying out beneath him.

He let his own intertwine with hers, squeezing just the slightest.

"Go to sleep, my sweet Avarice."

"When I was little, my mom used to

sing to me when I was sick. I miss her."

Cassius could feel the heat from her hand rising against his palm.

"I can only imagine." He sat next to her, the bed creaking only minimally.

Malcolm shifted in his chair at the sound, but he did not wake.

There was only the sound of her breath in the silence between them, and he thought for a moment she had fallen asleep.

"Seasons don't fear the reaper," her hazy voice whispered softly.

Cassius reached out softly, brushing her wet, sweat-slicked hair from her face.

"Nor do the wind, the sun, or the rain." His voice was strong and so full of hope, of love. If anyone would have heard it, they'd have handed him the stake themselves. But no one would hear this, no one would know, and there was the chance Ava herself would not remember this, but he would.

Ava curled closer to him, and Cassius didn't see anything else. He'd never see anything else and would never forget this stolen moment as long as he lived. Even if she woke up, thinking it was all a dream, for him, it would be enough.

It would be enough to get him through however long his sentence was.

"We can be like they are," she whispered, her breath warm on his skin, glassy eyes staring deeply into his, eyelashes fluttering before they closed once more.

"Don't fear the reaper." He didn't miss a beat, the words a prayer on his lips.

Ava's whispers turned inaudible, a

string of incoherent mumbles as she faded back into slumber.

Though, he knew the words quite well.

"Baby, I'm your man," he whispered to the darkness, a silent promise before he let go and disappeared into the shadows once more.

EPILOGUE

1 month later

AVA WATCHED THE television in the corner of the Third Eye, flipping through the channels. It was a slow day, and she had already stocked the shelves, rearranged the bookshelves. There was no excitement in Chester, not like there used to be. She stopped on a news station as reporters hounded a hooded figure that looked oddly familiar.

She read the caption below, "Sam Kingsley pulls long-awaited documentary and announces his last season of *Hell on Earth*. Fans are outraged."

"Well, that sucks, I was really looking forward to that," she grumbled. Her best friend, Ember, looked up from her tarot card spread, raising an eyebrow.

"Isn't that the guy you met at TerrorCon?" she asked.

"Yeah. We had a drink at the bar together. He was actually kind of nice."

"Did you two... you know..."

"Oh yeah." She nodded, waggling her eyebrows in response.

"You're pulling my leg..." Ember said with a blush.

"I'm not. It just kinda happened. Right before everyone came down with that awful food poisoning."

"I still can't believe that. What a time for food borne illness. All those people were sick for days, good lord. That really sucks when you have to spend the rest of your vacation sick, you know."

"Yeah, it definitely bites," Ava said as she set down the remote.

"Wanna read my cards?" she asked nonchalantly.

Ember nodded.

"Yeah, sure. I'm trying to learn some new spreads, so if you're up for experiments..." She shuffled her cards and Ava pushed off from the counter and headed toward the folding table Ember had taken residence at.

"All right, Miss Cleo, deal me."

Ember dealt the cards as Ava continued to watch the television. The news of the club responsible for the food poisoning, it looked like, had closed, the owner vanishing overnight, after a mysterious fire left the place burned to a crisp.

The camera panned over the landscape, showing the beautiful Silver Starling set against a stormy gray sky as they discussed what the media called "Con Crud."

Ember counted her cards, and the camera panned to an unsuspecting building with a large open window, yellow tables with hardly anyone inside sitting at them, behind the woman being interviewed, and Ava's stomach growled.

"Did you eat breakfast?" Ember asked as she placed her cards in a spread Ava didn't recognize.

"Not unless you count the venti caramel macchiato I woofed down in ten seconds on the way here."

"Want to get some lunch after this?" Ember asked as she placed the last card down.

Ava's phone vibrated in her pocket, drawing her attention away from her wandering thoughts.

"Actually, I could really go for a donut."

Ember smiled. "Cherry filled?"

Ava blinked, feeling the strangest sense of déjà vu, but she shrugged it off.

"No, red velvet supreme," she said as the news prattled on about the upcoming Chester Witch's Festival.

"Since when do you like red velvet anything? I thought you hated chocolate.”

“People change, I guess.”

Ember flipped over the first card.

“This is your situation, or what is going on with you right now,” she stated matter of factly.

Ava glanced down at the card, recognizing the imagery immediately.

The three of swords.

She knew the suit of swords well.

“Oh wait, I actually know this one,” she said excitedly.

Ember leaned back and motioned to her friend.

“Heartbreak, grief. Oversensitivity. Usually indicates turmoil in one’s love life.” Ava smiled smugly.

“Or a breakup.” Ember smirked.

“Ah, Em, that’s the trick. Can’t have a breakup if you don’t commit to anyone.”

She winked, letting out a small laugh.

Ember rolled her eyes.

"It could also just mean a separation. Maybe someone in your life is pulling back."

"Maybe." She nodded to Ember to pull the next card.

"What's the obstacle?"

"Are you doing this reading, or am I?" She teased.

"You." Ava batted her eyelashes sweetly at her friend.

"Then let me read." Ember continued to flip the card.

"The two of cups is your obstacle, and I'm reading that as upright," she stated positively.

Ava raised an eyebrow. She knew the cups was the suit of love. Coupled with a tragic card such as the three of swords, she couldn't help but feel annoyed.

Love was not something she had time for, something she sought. It wasn't as if she had the best track record. Every relationship she'd had seemed to fall into disaster.

Ross, dead by vampires.

Sam, romantic involvement thwarted by demon possession.

Dallas...

Ava shot the thought down immediately. There was nothing between her and Dallas. He'd proved that when he'd stayed silent for two years.

And then, there was Cassius.

The only man who remained a constant visual in her life wasn't a man at all.

He was a creature of the night.

A creature of blood and lust,

incapable of such human emotions as *love*.

Nothing would ever matter more to him than blood, and it was best she remembered that.

She'd only seen him once since returning from Oklahoma. He'd stopped by the Third Eye a week after her return with a cup of coffee. A coffee she needed desperately, since sleep was not her friend, lately.

The nightmares, it seemed, had only gotten worse since her trip to TerrorCon. She still relived the death of Ross, the sight of her parents. It seemed the memories of a painful bite, the glowing red glare of demonic eyes, waited for her in the dark and left her in a cold sweat with a racing heart.

And when she'd awakened to the cold

chill of the air with her stake in her hand, ready for the monsters, she found herself alone. And just as the terror of loneliness set in, the wind would blow and her skin would prickle with the slightest of goosebumps.

She'd wrap her arms around her legs and close her eyes and she'd whisper to the night, the words her mother would always sing to soothe her to sleep.

Seasons don't fear the reaper.

And on some nights, when exhaustion was too much to fight, she could swear the wind answered, "Nor do the wind, the sun, or the rain."

Ava & Cassius will be back in Blood & Ash. COMING SOON!

Turn the page now for a preview.

PREVIEW

"HARDER," AVA BREATHED as her back was slammed up against the wall. A sheen of sweat had already started to form on her skin, and her muscles were starting to ache, but she didn't care.

Dallas grunted in response, his hand around her throat.

"Is that all you've got?" she said with

a smirk. His fingers rested just above her jugular, and a part of her wanted to feel the force, the tight grip she knew he was capable of. Because in those moments, the ones that were far more frequent these days than they'd been before, she was free.

Free from the nightmares that plagued her.

Free from the ghosts that haunted her.

Well, the vampire who haunted her, really. Though, with the way Cassius appeared and disappeared at will like the wind, he was quite ghostlike at times.

Always there, watching.

Waiting.

Ava brought her lips to Dallas's, forcing the thoughts away. She could taste the saltiness of the sweat on his lip, the metallic taste of blood that hadn't quite dried yet from their last go-around in the ring, or more accurately, the mattress of Motel 6 that was acting as a boxing ring in place of the Bat Cave's comfortable gym.

"You drive me up a fucking wall, you know that?" Dallas bit back as he moved his lips from hers to her neck.

Ava started to feel lightheaded from all of it—the sparring, the secrecy, the memories, the feel of Dallas and all his hardened edges encompassing her.

Now was her chance.

She wrapped her legs around his waist, dragging her nails up his arm, fingers finding their way into his hair, twisting softly before tightening her grip.

She forcibly yanked his head to the

side, a wicked gleam in her eye.

"Oh, I know, Dallas. That's the fun of it," she said between breaths.

Dallas smiled devilishly back at her before breaking her tight hold, his eyes full of heat and desire.

Desire that she knew echoed in her own eyes, beneath her skin.

Her muscles ached, her head was splitting, and she was certain she'd be sore tomorrow, but she didn't care.

It was getting harder and harder to care, and a part of her almost *wished* the others would knock on the door, would find them tangled up together so that she could breathe again.

She hated lying to her brother, hated having to pretend everything was fine and nothing had changed, when, in fact, *everything* had changed.

Dallas slid his hands underneath her thighs, turning her around before slamming her back onto the mattress of messy sheets once more, his weight heavy on top of her.

Ava wriggled and writhed beneath him as his large hand held her wrists together, his grip firm. She moved around, twisting and turning, her breasts brushing against his sweat-soaked chest. In the amber light of the motel room, he looked like every dream, every fantasy, every bad decision a girl could ever dream of.

"Fight me, Ava," he growled, grinding his rigid length against her thigh.

She grunted and huffed in annoyance, her muscles tightening, her leg starting to go numb from the weight.

It wasn't all that different from the

first time they'd done this, four years ago. She could still remember how it felt when he wrapped his arms around her, held her close. How badly she'd wanted to submit and give into the temptation of Jake Dallas, even then.

But now…

"Jake," she whined, a strange feeling working its way up her body, through her blood, into her heart, her mind. The name rolled off her tongue all too easily, even though she rarely called him by his first name.

"I can't, I—" Her breath started to come in faster, and panic started to set in. Memories started to resurface, of the night she almost died.

The night Cassius saved her life.

The night it changed forever.

She was trapped, and there was no

way out.

"Fight me, Kitten. I know you can," he said, his voice strained, but yet, full of something she'd never heard before.

It would be so easy to just let go...

She remembered the feeling of emptiness in the dark, dank room she'd been left in.

The memory of Cassius's fangs in her wrist pushed forth, the familiar cyclone in her stomach.

The memory of the pure ecstasy she'd felt in that moment was a powerful memory, the hardest of them all to fight.

"I don't want to fight!" she bit back, tears starting to form behind her eyes.

Images of the golden-haired, green-eyed vampire filled her brain like an angry wave, trying to pull her under. Her heart started to race, the world around her spinning, and the force of it all was too strong.

The death of her parents.

The vampire killing Ross, her college boyfriend.

The incubus who'd she'd let into her body in more ways than one.

The taste of vampire blood on her lips from the spatter when she'd plunged her stake in their chest, and the smell of smoke from their decay.

Dallas loosened his grip but he did not let go. Instead his fingers entwined with hers in a soft gesture that felt foreign to her.

Dallas wasn't *soft* in any way of the word.

No, Dallas was a force of nature, a hurricane that would undoubtedly wreck her and destroy her into a million pieces.

But still, she wanted the wrath of his storm. She wanted to be caught up in the eye of all that he was, because death was not an option. As long as she wore Cassius's mark, death would one day come for her and she would not submit to it.

Not over her dead body.

"Ava," Dallas's voice turned softer, his free hand pushing her sweaty, wet strands of hair behind her ear.

When she looked up into his eyes, she could see her own fear reflected in them, and she hated it.

She hated herself for not being strong enough.

"Ava, I—" His thumb brushed her bottom lip, her heart racing.

The world around her started to fade back into reality, and she swallowed harshly.

"I can't do this right now," she said as she fought the tears.

Dallas was quiet for a moment, his gaze settling on her. He let go of her wrists, easing his weight off of her.

She expected him to just leave her alone. That was what he normally did when she'd been pushed too far; give her space to ground herself again. Training with Dallas was always like that. It always pushed her past her limits, because the intent was to be stronger than her fears. To be strong enough to survive vampire Jedi-mind tricks as well as to combat their strength. It was the difference between life and death, and it was familiar.

But the tears weren't.

"I don't know what happened, I just—"

Dallas wrapped his arms around her and pulled her into his lap, his fingers brushing along her arm in the gentlest of touches. He tilted her head up, and looked in her eyes in a way that was quite different than the other times. The heat, the lust had diminished and in its place was something far more dangerous.

Sympathy.

The touch felt...intimate.

Loving almost.

"Don't look at me like that," she said as she pushed him in the chest. Not hard enough to move him, though she could have if she wanted to.

"Like what?" he asked, his brows furrowing in concern.

Ava didn't like it.

"Like I'm some fucking damsel in

distress. I don't need your pity, I just… need a fucking break." She shoved him, and he fell back against the mattress, running his hand over his face.

"From this—" He motioned to the hotel room, which looked to be in disarray from their steamy 'sparring' session.

"Or…"

The words hit Ava like a brick as she considered them. She moved off the bed, snatching up her clothes on the floor that had come off at some point after the second round, when sweat and heat made them both uncomfortable.

Ava froze.

Before she could even speak, both of their phones started going off, rattling against the end table.

Dallas sighed, getting up from the

bed as she pulled on her Blue Oyster Cult shirt.

"It's Mal," Dallas said, turning to her.

She slid her jeans on slowly.

"Yeah, and?"

"Get your stake. We have a nest to infiltrate," he said the words plainly, as if they were the most normal thing in the world. As if the strange moment they'd just shared, the one where he *held* her, hadn't happened at all.

Maybe it's better if I just try and forget about it.

Forget about today, forget about whatever this is that's happening between us.

Ava nodded as she buttoned her jeans.

"Riding separately?" she asked, her nerves starting to settle.

Dallas stood there, the light of his phone illuminating him and his double star tattoos, the shadows falling on the planes of his chiseled jaw, his dark features.

"Of course." He nodded.

"All right. See you there," she said as she grabbed her phone, silencing it and sliding into her pocket before throwing on her leather jacket. She reached for the door, pausing for a moment.

It was just a moment, a split second of waiting as she realized Jake Dallas did nothing to stop her. He did not protest or beg her to stay.

Do I want him to?

She forced the question away as soon as it entered her brain.

No, I can't go down that road.

No, instead he let her walk out the

door without a sound into the crimson sunset.

Ava settled into her Impala, turning the keys in the ignition.

The familiar guitar strings of Heart's Magic Man filled the car, and Ava sighed as she backed out of the Motel 6 parking lot, speeding off for the highway. Off to hunt something she could catch.

Watch for Blood & Ash at your favorite online retailer.

OTHER BOOKS BY ARIEL DAWN

Speed Dating with the Denizens of the Underworld Series

Hecate

Hades

Orion

Ava Crowley, Vampire Slayer

<u>Blood & Bones</u>

Blood & Lust

Blood & Ash

The Hunter Games

Blood Of My Enemy

Blood Of The Lost

Blood Of My Love

Monsters Of Ashwood

<u>Voices In The Dark: A Monster Reverse
Harem Romance</u>

The Forevermore Series

In The Cards

In The Blood

In The Shadows

In The Deep

In The Garden

In The Night-coming soon!

Shifters Of Starfall Creek Series

Hollow's Sunrise

Hollow's Sunset

Hollow's Legacy

<u>Shifters of Starfall Creek Collection:</u>

<u>Books 1-3</u>

Get a copy of Ariel Dawn's short story, Faded, when you sign up for her newsletter!

<u>https://mailchi.mp/e5f326e433bf/dawn</u>

<u>-breaks-official-newsletter</u>

CONNECT WITH ARIEL DAWN

Website

http://www.ariel-dawn.com

Goodreads:

http://www.goodreads.com/authorarieldawn

Bookbub:

http://www.bookbub.com/authors/ariel-dawn

Facebook:

http://www.facebook.com/authorarieldawn

BLOOD & LUST

Twitter:

https://twitter.com/ArielDawn10

Join Dusk Chasers—Ariel Dawn's Official Readers Group for access to exclusive content!

ABOUT ARIEL DAWN

USA TODAY BESTSELLING AUTHOR Ariel Dawn grew up as an avid reader and is a creative soul.

What started out as writing reviews for indie romance authors led to featuring quirky, stereotypical, and weird covers on her Instagram Wrong Turn Romance, which gave her the courage to finally decide to live her dream and become an author.

Ariel writes plot driven paranormal romance and hopes to venture into fantasy and rom-com in the future. When she isn't writing, she can be found cosplaying, attending conventions, creating all sorts of artwork in her studio, or editing photos for her photography business.

A self-professed geek and foodie, she loves hanging out with family and friends and playing video games and board games with her retro gamer husband.